The on collisio ...top smashing against the guardrail

Swerving left long enough to disentangle the two vehicles, Bolan put his right foot on the brake, causing the Mustang to decelerate sharply.

The assassin's car continued to scrape against the guardrail for several seconds before the assassin also swerved left. But unlike the Executioner's maneuver, the assassin went too far and spun around counterclockwise. Tires squealed as the car went into an uncontrolled spin.

The truck didn't slow down.

Bolan slammed his foot on the brake, bringing his car to a screeching halt. The truck did likewise, but had considerably more momentum on its side, and so did not stop immediately.

Bolan watched as the truck smashed into the other car.

MACK BOLAN ®
The Executioner

The Executioner®
Don Pendleton's

DEEP RECON

A GOLD EAGLE BOOK FROM
W♦RLDWIDE®

TORONTO • NEW YORK • LONDON
AMSTERDAM • PARIS • SYDNEY • HAMBURG
STOCKHOLM • ATHENS • TOKYO • MILAN
MADRID • WARSAW • BUDAPEST • AUCKLAND

First edition June 2010

ISBN-13: 978-0-373-64379-0

Special thanks and acknowledgment to
Keith R. A. DeCandido for his contribution to this work.

DEEP RECON

Printed in U.S.A.

I do not love the bright sword for its sharpness, nor the arrow for its swiftness, nor the warrior for his glory. I only love that which they defend.

—J.R.R. Tolkien
(1892–1973)
The Two Towers

I will protect the people of this nation from all traitors, whether by gun, sword, arrow—or my bare hands.

—Mack Bolan

THE
MACK BOLAN
LEGEND

Nothing less than a war could have fashioned the destiny of the man called Mack Bolan. Bolan earned the Executioner title in the jungle hell of Vietnam.

But this soldier also wore another name—Sergeant Mercy. He was so tagged because of the compassion he showed to wounded comrades-in-arms and Vietnamese civilians.

Mack Bolan's second tour of duty ended prematurely when he was given emergency leave to return home and bury his family, victims of the Mob. Then he declared a one-man war against the Mafia.

He confronted the Families head-on from coast to coast, and soon a hope of victory began to appear. But Bolan had broken society's every rule. That same society started gunning for this elusive warrior—to no avail.

So Bolan was offered amnesty to work within the system against terrorism. This time, as an employee of Uncle Sam, Bolan became Colonel John Phoenix. With a command center at Stony Man Farm in Virginia, he and his new allies—Able Team and Phoenix Force—waged relentless war on a new adversary: the KGB.

But when his one true love, April Rose, died at the hands of the Soviet terror machine, Bolan severed all ties with Establishment authority.

Now, after a lengthy lone-wolf struggle and much soul-searching, the Executioner has agreed to enter an "arm's-length" alliance with his government once more, reserving the right to pursue personal missions in his Everlasting War.

Prologue

The autumn winds blew in off the Gulf of Mexico and kicked up outside the midnight black car. It was windy enough that the twenty-five-year-old car creaked and squeaked and even shook at times.

It didn't matter to Agent John McAvoy. He loved both the autumn season and his old retired police car, a 1982 Crown Victoria. There were better cars, but McAvoy loved things with problems and faults. He preferred to work with things and figure out what went wrong, then make them right. Often, he joked that that was why he married his ex-wife, only to learn that *things* could be fixed—people, not so much.

Back when he was a detective for the Chicago Police Department, McAvoy was that rarest of detectives who actually liked a good mystery, a stone-cold whodunit. McAvoy relished the cases his fellow detectives loathed. They all wanted the slam dunks, the easy arrests, where there was a reliable witness and plenty of physical evidence, plus minimum paperwork.

But not McAvoy. He wanted to solve things. It gave him a greater sense of accomplishment, the feeling of a job well done. That trait made him well-suited to the more complicated work done by the Bureau of Alcohol, Tobacco, Firearms and Explosives. He'd moved over to BATF after only ten years with CPD, having grown weary of Chicago's weather and politics, and having needed a change after his divorce. Not that the politics were any better in Florida—in fact, they were worse, as hard to believe as that was—but at least there was more sun and no winter.

Best of all, no ex-wife and a lot more pretty women. It definitely had been the right move.

It had been months on this particular undercover case. Last May, he'd become Donald Kincaid, a Key West–based gunrunner. It was miserable, cozying up to the scum of the Earth, having to pretend to be their pals. However, the months of work had gained him valuable information.

He hoped it would all be worth it.

McAvoy sat at his steering wheel, a burning cigarette dangling from between his lips, reading the file on a former Marine lieutenant turned gunrunner named Kevin Lee. The BATF agent had read it all before, of course—Lee was one of the major players in South Florida—but McAvoy couldn't get over Lee's impeccable service record with the Corps, ending with a tour in Afghanistan. He had no reprimands, no bad behavior, no warning signs at all—it was spotless. Sometimes, he thought, people just flipped a switch.

It had taken him months to get the lead on this warehouse. McAvoy was sure that he was close to the jackpot, finally—the light at the end of the tunnel that would get him back behind his desk at the BATF field office in Miami.

He could see men were wandering aimlessly in and

out of this warehouse on Stock Island, the penultimate of the islands that made up the Florida Keys, the last being Key West, the southernmost point in the continental United States.

McAvoy had parked his Crown Vic in the lot of a scuba diving place next door. The dive shop had several cars and SUVs present, as it was running a night dive, so McAvoy's car didn't stand out.

The warehouse was supposed to be shut down, but Kevin Lee had taken over the property through a shell company. That was the thing about illegal operations—nothing was legit or permanent.

Peering through his Bushnell 8x30 Imageview Instant Replay Binoculars, McAvoy saw that the guards were fairly lax. There were only two of them, and they patrolled the perimeter once every hour or so—if they even remembered. One was wearing an MP3 player, while the other had been paging through a skin magazine, occasionally holding it up for his music-listening partner to share in the joy of the airbrushed, Photoshopped, silicone-laden female form.

Their rifles were slung unceremoniously across their shoulders. McAvoy was seriously tempted to take the warehouse now, but he didn't have any backup. Using the Bushnell's five-megapixel camera, he took several more pictures, then checked the memory.

The only thing he still needed was Lee himself. If he'd enter the building, and McAvoy got a picture of him doing so, that, along with all the other intel he'd gathered, would be enough probable cause for a warrant to hit the warehouse.

McAvoy's plan was to wait until the night dive ended, and leave along with the other cars in the lot. If Lee hadn't shown up by then, he'd try again tomorrow night. He'd been at this for months, and while he was eager to close the case, he was equally eager to do it right. It wouldn't do after all this to get tripped up on some picayune piece of procedure just because he was in a rush to stop being Kincaid.

Moments later, as he was ashing his cigarette out the rolled-down window, he saw movement near his Crown Vic, and his plan suddenly changed.

McAvoy knew that whoever was out there would be easier dealt with in the open space of the parking lot. He put out his cigarette in the car's ashtray and just as he was about to reach into the well between the seats where he kept his Walther PPK .380 a voice sounded from the passenger side.

"I wouldn't move, if I were you Mr. Kincaid."

The voice belonged to Kevin Lee.

"Or, rather," Lee continued, "should I say Agent McAvoy?"

The BATF agent's blood froze. He'd been so careful, worked so hard for months. How the hell had his cover been blown?

Still, he had to keep it up for as long as he could, especially since the other person he'd seen moving was now fully visible outside the driver's door. It was one of Lee's goons—a bulky Cuban named Jiminez—pointing a police-issue Glock 17 right at McAvoy's head.

"Kevin? The hell're you doin' here? I'm just waitin' on Lola, she's supposed to be back from her freakin' night-dive by now." His partner in this undercover was a former Monroe County Sheriff's Office deputy turned freelance operative named Lola Maxwell, and her cover was as a woman who, among other things, loved to scuba dive.

"For an undercover BATF agent, you don't play dumb very well, Agent McAvoy. I was hoping that it wouldn't come to this. But I suppose that's how it has to be." Lee nodded to Jiminez.

At the same time as the nod, McAvoy threw his shoulder to his left, the metal of the suddenly open door slamming into Jiminez's midsection, denying him the opportunity to pull the trigger.

McAvoy rolled out of the car on his left shoulder, coming up on one knee. He hadn't had the chance to grab his Walther out of the car, and Jiminez was still holding his Glock.

McAvoy wasn't worried about Lee. Despite having led a rifle company in Afghanistan—or perhaps because he had—Lee never carried. That was what he had goons like Jiminez for.

Pivoting on the leg whose foot was flat on the ground, McAvoy rose and thrust his other foot out toward Jiminez, catching the large Cuban in the solar plexus.

Jiminez doubled over, trying to catch his breath. With someone as big and well-muscled as the Cuban, you had to go for something that would hurt no matter who you were. One place was the solar plexus, where a good hit would knock the wind out of you.

Of course, McAvoy had actually been aiming for his balls. That always worked, too. But he kicked too high.

Unlike slamming the door into the Cuban's body, kicking him in the stomach got him to drop the Glock. McAvoy snatched at it, even as a bullet whistled loudly by his head from behind.

Whirling, he saw another one of Lee's guys—the Samoan guy, whose name McAvoy didn't know, but everyone called him "Pooky" for some reason. The man was holding a Desert Eagle .50 Action Express, pointed right at where McAvoy's head had been before he dived for the Glock.

The Desert Eagle had serious recoil, so it was hard to squeeze off multiple rapid-fire rounds. Gripping the Glock with both hands and turning so he was sitting on the ground and leaning against his Crown Vic to prevent his own recoil issues, the agent fired off six rounds.

Or, rather, tried to. The weapon jammed after the third shot. McAvoy aimed unpleasant thoughts at people who didn't maintain their weapons.

One of the Glock's bullets had sliced through Pooky's left arm, shredding bone and muscle and cartilage. Blood had exploded from the wound, dripping onto the asphalt of the parking lot.

Unfortunately, Pooky was right handed, so he still held the Desert Eagle. And he didn't even flinch from the bullet wound. McAvoy wasn't sure if that was because Pooky was tough or because Pooky had more heroin than blood flowing through his veins.

The Samoan squeezed off another shot from the Desert Eagle one-handed, and stumbled backward from the recoil.

McAvoy only barely registered Pooky's issues, though, as the .50-caliber round tore into his left thigh, pulverizing arteries and veins, destroying flesh and shattering bone. Blood gushed from the wound, and McAvoy realized with certainty that his femoral artery had been hit.

Blinking away the tears of pain that welled up in his eyes, he managed to clear the misfire and squeeze off another shot with the Glock, one that went right between the Samoan's eyes.

That, though, was his swan song. He could feel the life draining out of him, his limbs growing weaker and weaker, his thoughts getting fuzzier, his vision getting cloudier. The only thing that remained vivid and constant was the agonizing pain emanating from his destroyed left leg.

The last thing Agent John McAvoy of the Bureau of Alcohol, Tobacco, Firearms and Explosives would ever hear was Kevin Lee saying the words, "Goodbye, John."

LOLA MAXWELL wasn't on the dive boat, of course. She was in a bar on Duval Street, clutching the same pint of beer she'd been nursing for over an hour, wondering where the hell McAvoy was.

He had said he would call her when he was back home, which would be after the night dive at the shop next to Lee's warehouse. But that dive had started at eight o'clock and was scheduled to end at nine-thirty. True, the water was choppy, so the dive might have run late, but surely not more than forty-five minutes or so. It was only a five- or ten-minute drive back from Stock Island to Johnny's bungalow on Eaton Street.

Which meant that Lola should have heard from him no later than a quarter to eleven or so. It was now creeping toward eleven-thirty.

There was a band playing cover tunes at the front of the bar, and they started playing "Brown-Eyed Girl" for the third time that night. That, combined with worry over John and lack of desire to continue being hit on by drunks, caused her to gulp down the remainder of her beer and depart.

She had a bad feeling about all of this.

When she came out onto Duval Street, the autumn

breeze cutting through her shoulder-length red hair, she pulled out her cell phone, hoping that maybe she hadn't heard the chirp of the ringer over the din of the cover band.

But there were no messages, no missed calls, no sign of Johnny.

As she ambled quickly down the sidewalk, expertly weaving her way around drunken college students and the like, she called Jean-Louis, her "associate"—a euphemistic term for extra muscle, in both the physical and firepower departments—in the hopes that Johnny might have contacted him.

"No can do, Lo," he said. There was a lot of noise in the background, so Jean-Louis was probably at the Cutter's Wharf, his preferred watering hole.

"I'm going to the warehouse."

Jean-Louis hesitated. "You sure that's such a good idea, boss?"

Lola snorted. Jean-Louis only called her "boss" when he was trying to talk her out of something. "I know it's a bad idea, Jean-Louis, but in six months, he's never missed a scheduled call-in. He'd only miss one if something awful had happened—I have to know."

Minutes later, she'd arrived at her own bungalow on Whitehead Street, her cherry-red, fully restored 1965 Mustang convertible in the driveway. Sliding the key into the driver's door, she slid into the seat and turned over the 289 2V engine.

Purring like a happy cat being scratched behind the neck, the engine went smoothly into reverse at Lola's moving of the gearshift.

This late at night, the traffic was fine on Whitehead, and moving decently on Route 1 to the bridge, though it seemed agonizingly slow to Lola.

A pit opened up in the bottom of her stomach as she turned off Route 1 onto the side road that led to the dive shop, the warehouse and the restaurant across the street.

But Lola saw none of those things. She saw only the flashing lights and the yellow crime-scene tape.

Dozens of sedans and SUVs were parked, all with the rapid-fire sequence of colored lights that indicated they belonged to law enforcement. There were people wearing the uniform of the Monroe County Sheriff's Office, and plainclothes agents wearing windbreaker jackets with "BATF" stenciled in big white letters on the back.

The tape cordoned off both the warehouse and the dive shop.

The pit in Lola's stomach grew wider.

She parked the Mustang and managed to talk to Deputy Hobart, who'd always had the hots for her, into letting her past the tape.

Several agents were standing over two dead bodies, using various pieces of crime-scene investigation equipment. One victim was a giant of a man, wounded in both the forehead and left arm, the former likely to have been the fatal shot. But Lola barely noticed that, instead focusing on the one with the mangled left thigh: Agent John McAvoy.

"Noooo!" Lola cried out as she raced toward the body, her eyes welling with tears.

One of the agents stopped her, wrapping his arms around her in a bear hug that kept her arms at her side.

"Let me go!"

Another agent stared hard at her. "Who the hell are you, lady? And what are you doing in my crime scene?"

"My name is Lola Maxwell—I was working with Johnny—with Agent McAvoy." Then she remembered the password Johnny had given her in case she ever found herself speaking to a BATF agent about this case. "Galleria."

The agent blinked twice, then looked at the person manhandling Lola. "Let her go."

After she was free, Lola knelt so she could see Johnny better, years of training keeping her from actually disturbing the body and any evidence it might contain. It looked like his thigh had been hit by a large-caliber bullet that shredded the femoral artery. He would've bled out in moments.

The other body meant that nothing would come of it from an investigative standpoint. The Samoan—who looked like one of Lee's goons, the one they called Pooky—killed the BATF agent, and the BATF agent killed Pooky. Lola had been a cop too long to know that this was just two murders that had conveniently solved each other. The paperwork would be clean and easy, the cases would improve the county's crime stats, and life would go on. No one would avenge Johnny's death because they knew who killed him.

Her heart ached from the sight of his glass-eyed stare, but she vowed that she would carry on, the cold fire of vengeance burning behind her tear-filled eyes.

1

The satellite phone had interrupted Mack Bolan's fishing.

Strictly speaking, that wasn't entirely true. He'd been on a rented boat in the middle of Bear Lake near Atlanta, Michigan, all day, but not a single salmon had taken the bait at the end of his line. Was it really fishing if you didn't catch any fish?

Bolan rarely took downtime, as there was always something that needed his attention. He valued his R and R, and he was a practical man. He had never subscribed to the notion that the rest and relaxation was the most important part of fishing. If one wanted to rest and relax, there were plenty of ways to do it, and he wouldn't have had to leave his rented cabin or take the small motorboat into the middle of Bear Lake.

No, he wanted to fish. But the salmon weren't exactly cooperating.

The Executioner took very few vacations, but it was time for him to kick back and clear his mind, take time so that his body could heal from all that he'd put it through in the past few weeks.

But he'd been in Montmorency County for twenty-four hours, and he was bored, so he quickly snatched up the sat phone when it signaled an incoming call.

"Striker," the gruff voice of Hal Brognola said, "sorry to interrupt your time off, but it's been twenty-four hours, so I assume you're ready to go back to work?"

Brognola knew him well. "What's the mission?"

"There'll be a Stony Man plane on the tarmac at Atlanta Municipal Airport within the hour to take you to Key West International Airport. The full mission brief will be there."

"Anything else?"

"It'll all be in the intel package. Let me know if you need anything else."

Bolan disconnected with Brognola after his goodbyes and steered the boat back to the shore.

It took fifty minutes to return the boat, pack his few things into a duffel, check out of the cabin, and take his rental car to the airport, where he returned it. Stony Man had sent a private jet just as Brognola had promised. Bolan could see Charlie Mott, one of Stony Man's pilots, waiting on the tarmac.

Bolan went easily through security, his credentials allowing him to bring his 9 mm SIG-Sauer P-226 handgun into the airport without question. He had only the one weapon—he was, technically, on vacation, after all.

Boarding the plane, he saw that Brognola had antici-pated his needs, as usual. An ICC aluminum case covered in black ballistic nylon sat on one of the eight comfortable chairs, and a Pelican 1780W HL Long Case on another. A quick look revealed they held a Mark XIX Desert Eagle .357 Magnum pistol and an RRA Tactical Entry 5.56 mm automatic rifle, respectively. On one of the two seats opposite where the weaponry had been placed was a laptop.

Mott quietly closed the door to the plane and clambered into the cockpit. "We'll be in the air in two shakes, Striker. Nice to have you aboard."

"Thanks, Charlie. Good to see you again."

Taking the seat next to the laptop after stowing his duffel, the Executioner picked it up and opened it, settling it on his lap while the machine left standby mode.

The laptop's desktop—which was from a proprietary operating system created by Aaron "the Bear" Kurtzman, Stony Man's computer expert—had only one folder visible on it, simply labeled Striker. Bolan double-clicked on it.

For the rest of the trip south, Bolan read through every file in that folder. The latest in a series of attempts by the Bureau of Alcohol, Tobacco, Firearms and Explosives to get close to a Key West–based gunrunner named Kevin Lee had failed, a long-term undercover agent named John McAvoy had been found dead near an empty warehouse. According to McAvoy's partner, an operative named Lola Maxwell, McAvoy had believed the warehouse to be one of Lee's main stashes for illegal weaponry he wanted to move, but McAvoy was made, and the warehouse cleaned out. The forensics report from the warehouse didn't provide any useful evidence. And a dead body was left behind to take the rap.

McAvoy had gotten much deeper than any previous undercover operative. His identity was known only to his handler, who had specifically been given autonomy to pick his own agent in the hopes of avoiding a leak. Still, he was made and executed.

BATF had a leak. Bolan's job was to find the leak and plug it once and for all.

Bolan knew both Maxwell and McAvoy by reputation. The latter was a solid agent with a good record, including an impressive bust of an operation working out of Chicago during his days as a CPD detective, after which BATF recruited him. He would be sorely missed.

Maxwell was more of a wild card. A sheriff's deputy in Monroe County, Florida, she moved on to the CIA and then became a freelance operative much like Bolan himself, though with less latitude, secrecy, or support than Bolan enjoyed. The CIA let her go for reasons undisclosed, at a time when the presidency changed hands from one political party to another. That meant that either she screwed up in such a way that was embarrassing to the company, or it was a political move by a new commander in chief putting his mark on things. Or, possibly, both.

According to the memo from Brognola that led off the documents in the file folder, Bolan was to work with Maxwell to uncover the leak and put Lee away. The higher-ups at BATF were not thrilled about it, according to Brognola, but knew that they had to get their own house in order first.

After the plane landed smoothly on the short runway at Key West's small airport—it received the rather outré designation of Key West International Airport by virtue of its proximity to Central and South America—Bolan took the two cases, but left the laptop. He'd tapped the special key that would wipe the hard drive.

In the small waiting area near the two small baggage claim stations Bolan spotted a large man with a round, bald head, huge arms that ended in wide shoulders, a barrel chest, squat legs, and no discernible neck, who seemed to have spotted him, also. Despite the man's size, Bolan couldn't detect an ounce of fat on him—easily done, as he was wearing a skintight muscle shirt and shorts. The Executioner noticed that the large man walked with a slightly odd gait and his right arm stuck out a bit farther from his side than his left. He was a man who was used to walking with a shoulder holster, and who didn't have it on because airport security would've been all over him.

Bolan readied himself as the man walked toward him. If this guy was one of Lee's men, it didn't bode well for this assignment. An op that began with a fire-fight five minutes after Bolan landed meant big trouble. Also, any leak had to have been tugboat-size if the Executioner's own involvement was known by his target only a couple hours after he got the mission.

The man walked up to Bolan and said, "Are you Mr. Cooper? I'm Mr. Faraday. I'm here to take you to Lola."

"Any particular reason why I should believe you?" Bolan asked.

Faraday was now standing close to Bolan. He was half a head shorter than the Executioner, but twice as wide. Still, Bolan had taken down bigger opponents unarmed, and he had his SIG-Sauer handy if he needed it. For that matter, he had two solid gun cases, one in either hand, both of which would make excellent blunt instruments should the need arise.

Then Faraday whispered the word "Galleria."

From his airplane reading, Bolan knew that was the BATF code word for McAvoy's op. In and of itself, it didn't prove as much as Faraday probably thought it did. If there was a leak, then McAvoy's code word might well have been common knowledge in Lee's organization.

Plus, Faraday's name appeared nowhere in that same airplane reading, which had included a full dossier on Lola Maxwell.

Still and all, Bolan was willing to go along with

Faraday for the time being, if for no other reason than
to gather information.

He followed Faraday out to the sun-drenched parking
lot, where he led them to a 1965 Mustang convertible.

Bolan's hopes for this mission continued to plummet.
A cherry-red Mustang was hardly the most inconspicuous vehicle to be using for an undercover op. And if it
was part of Maxwell's cover, should she really have
sent it out to pick him up?

Faraday squeezed his massive frame into the
Mustang, which also went some way toward explaining
the choice of car: Faraday's bulk would not have fit
comfortably in a more modern sedan. Of course, sedans
were hardly the only option, and the prevalence of SUVs
made that a far more inconspicuous mode of transport.

Bolan slid quietly into the passenger seat after
placing his duffel and gun cases in the backseat. As
Faraday drove out onto a road that ran alongside the
Gulf of Mexico, Bolan saw that this was hardly the only
vintage car around. That mitigated the problem, but
hardly solved it.

Gazing past Faraday's head, Bolan looked out and
saw the bright blue sky, broken by the occasional white
cloud, the sun's brightness doubled by reflecting off
the blue-with-whitecaps water of the Gulf. The water
was also filled with boats of all kinds, ranging from
small yachts to sailboats to motorboats very similar to
the one he was using for fishing in Michigan earlier this
day. Other, smaller boats were used to drag parasailers
through the sky.

The road came to an L intersection, and the Mustang
continued on it, turning right. Faraday navigated
through several other streets, which contained various

houses colored in pastels. A large number were new construction, due to the devastation wrought by Hurricane Katrina, though Bolan noted that they were still in the same style as the ones that were constructed in the nineteenth century when Key West was a major port of call and the wrecking industry was at its peak.

The Mustang pulled into the driveway of a bungalow on Whitehead Street. It was white with blue trim.

Before going inside, Bolan removed his Desert Eagle from its case, assembling it in just a few moments.

"You ain't gonna need that," Faraday said.

The Executioner said nothing, but continued to put his weapon together. He saw no reason to take Faraday at his word.

When the Desert Eagle was placed snugly in his waistband, reducing the SIG-Sauer in his shoulder holster to the status of backup weapon, Bolan said, "Let's go."

Inside the bungalow was sparsely furnished and lit by garish tropical daylight. Under the right circumstances, such bland décor and intense natural light could be used to disorient, but this was southern Florida, where bright sun was the order of the day.

Inside was a tall woman in her early- to mid-thirties with red shoulder-length hair and stunning emerald-green eyes. She wore a tube top that barely contained a sizable chest, flip-flops, and toenail polish that were all the same red as the Mustang. Her denim cutoffs had a belt holster that contained a Beretta U22 NEOS 22LR pistol.

"Lola Maxwell, I presume?" Bolan asked.

"That would be me. My contacts said you were the best. I've never known them to be wrong.

"We're trying to bring down a gunrunner here, Mr. Cooper, one who killed a BATF deep-cover agent."

"Yes, I know. I read the file. What I don't know is what you and your thug over here have to do with any of this."

Faraday tensed at the "thug" reference, but calmed at a look from Maxwell.

"Jean-Louis is my associate. He used to be an enforcer for a drug crew out of Key Largo, until I put him away. He's been working for me since he did his time."

"And you?"

"Since I left the CIA—"

Bolan almost smiled. "Since the CIA kicked you out on your ass, you mean. Don't screw around with me, Ms. Maxwell. I take on jobs that need to be done, and I can't do it with incompetents working alongside me."

"I'm not incompetent!" Maxwell said. "My leaving the CIA was political. I'm sure you know all about that."

"Yes, which is why I avoid politics."

"In any case, BATF hired me to provide support for Johnny—for Agent McAvoy on his undercover job."

Jerking a thumb toward Faraday, Bolan asked, "And he fits in where?"

"He helps me out," Maxwell said evasively, staring at the floor. "Look, it's easier to do this kind of thing if you have some kind of local talent. Jean-Louis and I know a lot of the players, plus we have deniability with BATF. Anyone digs, they'll find an ex-con and an ex-spook. My current work is completely off the grid—kinda like yours, I presume." She added that with an ironic smile. "And we're wasting time. I think I know who might've fingered Johnny."

Bolan folded his arms over his chest. He didn't like this. "How long were the two of you sleeping together?"

Maxwell blinked. "What are you talking about?" Her attempt at ignorance was pathetic.

Moving toward the door, the Executioner said, "We're done."

"What?"

"You slept with your partner. You're working with an ex-con. And I get the feeling you're more interested in vengeance for your lover's murder than in justice against a gunrunner. I appreciate the lift from the airport, but I'll take it from here by myself. Like I said before, I don't work with incompetents."

Bolan put his hand on the front doorknob when Maxwell said, "Wait!"

Turning, Bolan asked, "For what? You're not going to convince me that this op is anything but botched from the start. You're too close emotionally, and that clouds judgment—people end up dead. I don't want one of those people to be me, so we're done."

"But I told you, I know who fingered Johnny."

That got Bolan's hand off the doorknob—temporarily. "Why didn't you tell the BATF agents at the scene this?"

"Because I wasn't thinking straight at the scene. I've had a day to think about it, and I know who it has to be— Kenny V. The V is short for Valentino, his last name, but a lot of the boys call him Hot Lips."

"A good kisser?" Bolan asked.

"No," Maxwell said. "No, they call him that 'cause his lips are always flapping, and the boys all think that his mouth'll catch fire, they flap so fast."

"If he's that good a talker, how is he still alive?"

"He doesn't just talk well, he hears everything and knows everybody. He always makes deals that are good for both parties, and he never squeals."

"Time to break that streak, then," Bolan said, confident in his ability to extract information. "Where is he?"

"A bar on Sugarloaf Key called Micky's. He practically lives at the corner table between the jukebox and the pool table. We can be there in twenty minutes."

"No, *I* can be there in twenty minutes. I work better alone."

"Dammit, Cooper, you don't know the players, and you don't know the territory." She chuckled. "And look at you. You stand out like a sore thumb."

"Maybe. But I can't do my job and babysit you two. So stay here." Looking at Faraday, he said, "Car keys."

Faraday looked confused.

Glowering at Maxwell, Bolan said, "You want my help, we do things my way, and that means I go alone with no chance of you two following. I either take your car, or I slash the tires and go rent one of my own. Pick one."

Maxwell bit her lower lip, then nodded toward Faraday, who handed over the Mustang's keys.

"Smart choice." Bolan departed the bungalow.

The Mustang's engine turned over as soon as Bolan applied the key. The old car hummed like the well-oiled machine it was, and the Executioner was silently impressed with at least one aspect of Maxwell's character: she kept this four-decade-old car in pristine shape.

Once he'd put some distance between himself and Maxwell's bungalow, he took out his sat phone, which was also equipped with a GPS and a secure Internet connection. The latter enabled him to quickly obtain the precise address of Micky's on Sugarloaf Key, and the former provided directions.

Sure enough, it took almost exactly twenty minutes to get there. Bolan found a parking lot belonging to a bowling alley a block away from Micky's, and he parked the rather distinctive Mustang there.

The Executioner played a serious game, one with his life on the line constantly, and he would only trust someone he could count on to back him up. Every indication showed that Maxwell and her "associate" didn't qualify.

He pulled his jacket around him closer as he walked toward Micky's. The sun was setting and the temperature was plummeting. The wind that came in off the Atlantic was bitter and cut through Bolan.

Micky's was a large shack that probably had been used for storage once upon a time. From a distance it looked fairly rickety, and Bolan wondered how it survived hurricane season. But as he got closer, he saw evidence of steel reinforcement. A battered sign gave the name of the place, and what few windows there were were frosted over.

This area of Florida specialized in open-air eateries and drinkeries, and for a place to be this enclosed bespoke a certain illegality.

As if to reinforce that, Bolan walked through the thick metal door to find his nostrils assaulted with cigarette smoke. There were few interior public spaces left that allowed smoking, and while Bolan wasn't completely up on the Florida State code, he was fairly certain that bars in this state qualified. Places like this, though, bars that catered to the scum of humanity, tended to be smoke-filled throwbacks to a bygone era, a testament to how little the criminal element had changed.

The bar floor was nowhere near large enough to cover the full space of the building. In and of itself that didn't say much: the Florida Keys weren't structurally sound enough geologically to support much by way of basements, so the bar's storage facilities were probably aboveground. Still, Bolan was sure there was more than liquor stored in the area he couldn't see.

Bolan strode in like he owned the place, heading straight for a wooden stool at the bar. With a single glance he took in the interior: a bar along the left wall, a bartender standing behind it drawing the tap for a customer who sat at the far end, and a floor with a lot of wooden tables. While most of those tables had one or two men sitting at it—there wasn't a single woman in the place—the one between the jukebox and the pool table was empty.

So much for "practically living there." Bolan was running out of patience with Lola Maxwell already, and the op was less than twenty-four hours old.

He ordered the lightest beer they had. The bartender glared at him, and Bolan glared right back.

"You a cop?" the bartender asked.

Assuming a cover identity without a moment's hesitation, Bolan spoke in a New York accent. "Jesus H., is that a stupid question, or what? You really think I'm gonna just say, 'Yeah, I'm a cop'? I swear to Christ, the sun must bake your brains down here."

"When'd you come down from the Big Apple?" the bartender then asked with a smile.

Florida was filled with transplanted New Yorkers, so the accent wouldn't be hard for a bartender to place, but Bolan's cover required him to play dumb. "What makes you think I'm from New York? And we don't call it 'the Big Apple,' either, asshole."

"Look, maybe you'll want to try one of the places out on Route 1."

"Yeah? Kenny V hang out there, too?"

The bartender frowned. "You're here to see Hot Lips?"

"Christ, you don't really call him that, do ya?"

At that, the bartender smiled. "I'll get your drink."

As the bartender pulled the tap for the light beer, the door opened to the sound of someone talking a mile a minute.

"So I says to the bitch, I says, 'Hey look, bitch, if you don't wanna be doin' the deed, then you shouldn't'a been all cozyin' up to me like you was.' And she was sayin', 'I thought we was just dancin',' and I told her, 'Yo, bitch, when you dance with your cootchie all up against my leg, my guess is that you wanna be doin' more than dancin', you feel me?'"

That had to be Kenny Valentino. He had a shaved head, a chin beard and a gold tooth on the left side of his mouth. He seemed to be talking to himself, but as he entered Micky's, Bolan could see the wireless phone device in his left ear.

"I'm at the joint now, I gotta bounce. Hey, tell Delgado that Lee owes me, a'ight? Good. Peace."

He tapped the side of his wireless device, then signaled the bartender. "Yo, Marty! Draw me a beer!"

Marty, the bartender, nodded as he brought Bolan his beer. "That," Marty said to Bolan, "is the guy you're looking for."

"No kidding," Bolan said sardonically. "Kinda worked that out on my own, know what I'm sayin'?" He also was starting to understand where the Hot Lips nickname came from, if he was blithely mentioning Lee's name over an unsecured mobile phone line.

Kenny said hello to pretty much everyone in the bar, and engaged them in quick conversations. Though "conversations" may have been the wrong word, since none of the people other than Kenny actually said anything.

There were only two people Kenny didn't acknowledge. One was Bolan. The other was the man at the far end of the bar whom Marty had been serving when Bolan came in.

Bolan paid close attention to all the exchanges, especially the one between Kenny and a short, overweight Latino gentleman with pockmarked skin. After Kenny acknowledged him, the Latino looked right at the man at the end of the bar.

That man then got up and went over to Kenny.

The world seemed to move in slow motion for just a second. Bolan immediately noticed the bulge of a handgun. As the man reached under his windbreaker, Bolan leaped up from his own stool and ran toward the man, reaching for his Desert Eagle.

Even as Bolan moved, the man pulled out a Smith & Wesson .38-caliber handgun.

"What the f—" were Kenny's last words, as the man squeezed the trigger four times, putting each shot in Kenny Valentino's chest. The first bullet ripped into his chest, instantly pulverizing his heart. The subsequent three shots, which shredded his lungs, ribs and esophagus, were unnecessary, as the .38-caliber round tore the aorta to pieces, beyond the ability of even the finest hospital to repair.

A cacophony of voices exploded in the bar.

"Shit!"

"He killed Valentino!"

"Shoot the bastard!"

"I never liked the little asshole."

Pointing his Desert Eagle at the man's head, Bolan said, "Drop it now."

The man dived under the pool table. Bolan fired two rounds at the table, the .357 rounds blowing massive holes and sending splintered wood and pulverized felt everywhere.

As Bolan ran toward the pool table, the man popped up, now holding a second S&W .38 and firing both as he ran toward the door.

The Executioner was forced to dive for cover as bullets whizzed over his head.

The other men in the bar—including the pockmarked Latino who had signaled the assassin—had mostly moved toward the exits. Apparently, no one thought highly enough of Kenny Valentino to avenge his death.

Except for the Executioner. Valentino had survived all this time by being useful to the right people. Now, just when Bolan was about to talk to him about his role in informing on a federal agent, a professional showed up to put four bullets into him.

On the one hand, it meant that Bolan was on the right track. On the other, it meant that he couldn't question the man.

The shots stopped, and Bolan clambered to his feet, running to the front door.

Valentino's assassin was getting into a white Chevrolet Aveo, which made it much like every other car in south Florida.

Bolan risked throwing a shot, which would require him to steady his stance. Being light on your feet was not a blessing when you fired a .357 Magnum. He felt the tremendous recoil from the Desert Eagle vibrate through his entire body as the bullet sliced through the air, but he held his ground, his feet planted firmly in what martial artists called a three-point stance: one foot slightly in front of the other, toes inverted toward each other, knees bent, center of gravity dropped. It was one of the most stable stances possible, and people who mastered it couldn't be easily knocked down. Bolan had long ago achieved such mastery.

The round pulverized the back window of the Aveo, which shattered in an ear-splitting explosion of glass. The Executioner also saw shreds of leather and padding, indicating that the round had gone through one of the seats as well.

Bolan had obviously missed the assassin, as he then started the car and drove off. Even a glancing shot from a .357 round would leave someone unable to operate a motor vehicle.

As he ran as fast as he could down the street to where he'd parked Maxwell's Mustang, Bolan took some solace in the fact that he'd blown out the rear window of the Aveo, which would make it easier to pick up on the road.

Keeping his eye on the vehicle for as long as he could, Bolan saw it turn left at the end of the road, which meant the assassin was heading for the Overseas Highway— U.S. Route 1, the only road that traversed all the Keys. That was a mixed blessing. It meant that the assassin hadn't stashed a boat here on Sugarloaf Key, which meant Bolan could keep tailing him. But it also meant that the Executioner had to catch up to him before he reached Route 1, otherwise he wouldn't know whether he went south toward Key West or north toward mainland Florida.

As he approached the Mustang, Bolan leaped into the driver's seat, grateful that he'd left the top down. Sliding the key into the ignition, the Executioner knew he was about to find out how well Maxwell maintained her vintage vehicle.

Apparently, she did so very well. The '65 Mustang accelerated smoothly and quickly, and Bolan soon found himself behind a white Chevrolet Aveo with no back window that was turning left onto Crane Boulevard toward Route 1.

The Aveo was a solid, reliable car, often used by rental car companies, but never by car enthusiasts who preferred speed over function. So all things being equal, Bolan would have no trouble keeping up with the assassin with Maxwell's Mustang.

But all things were somewhat unequal, as there were other cars on the road, and for all that it had the designation of "boulevard," Crane was just a two-lane road.

Heedless of driving regulations, and common sense, the assassin weaved his Aveo in and out of his side and the oncoming-traffic side, almost getting clipped by vehicles any number of times.

When they reached Route 1, the Aveo swerved more than turned left through a red light. Bolan did likewise. The Executioner had been hoping that the Aveo would have gone right, and south toward Key West. There was a U.S. Navy station on Boca Chica Key, and the Executioner knew that facility well. He also could possibly have called upon some backup from the sailors on the ground there.

But instead, the assassin went north.

The Overseas Highway was also two lanes, which meant that traffic moved only as fast as the slowest person on the road. Paying no heed to other cars, the Aveo zipped in and out of lanes, clipping some vehicles. Bolan wasn't sure if he did so to increase his speed, or in the hopes that one of the cars he hit would interfere with Bolan's own ability to keep up, but if it was the

latter, it didn't work. The Mustang turned on the proverbial dime, and Bolan was easily able to avoid the
other cars on the road.

They continued over Summerland Key and into Big
Pine Key, his quarry continuing to treat the Overseas
Highway as his own personal slalom course.

When they reached the Seven Mile Bridge, a stretch
that traversed the Gulf of Mexico over the eponymous
distance between Little Duck Key and Key Vaca, the
traffic lessened—only the Mustang and the Aveo were
on this stretch. Bolan wasn't sure how long this would
last, but he would take advantage of the lack of innocent
bystanders and the distraction they posed.

About a mile onto the bridge, the assassin stuck an arm
out the driver's window and pointed the muzzle of his
S&W in Bolan's direction and squeezed off three shots.

None of them connected, as the assassin swerved
and rubbed up against the concrete railing that kept
drivers from going over the edge into the Gulf of
Mexico. Sparks flew as the passenger side ground
against the guardrail. The assassin righted the car soon
enough, but the slowdown from the friction and the
swerving allowed the Executioner to close the distance
between them.

He didn't rear-end the Aveo—that was a zero-sum
strategy. With two cars of roughly equal size, the rear-
ender always got it worse than the rear-endee. In this
case, the impact would severely damage the Mustang's
grille and have almost no effect on the Aveo's bumper.

Instead, Bolan took advantage of the presently nonexistent traffic to get into the northbound lane and pull
up alongside the Aveo.

The assassin tried to fire his .38 again. But before he

could get a shot off, Bolan swerved right, counting on the more solidly built 1965 car to be able to withstand the impact better than the much lighter and flimsier modern vehicle.

Again the Aveo ground against the concrete railing. Bolan saw the other man struggle to keep the steering wheel under control—and fail miserably. The Aveo was being crushed between the irresistible force of the barricade and the solidly built Mustang.

Headlights then shone in Bolan's face as a truck came into view going southbound on Route 1. The Mustang was still halfway into the southbound lane, and the only way to avoid a collision was to stop smashing the Aveo against the guardrail.

Swerving left long enough to disentangle the two vehicles from each other—which happened with another screech of metal against plastic—Bolan then put his right foot on the brake, causing the Mustang to decelerate sharply.

The Aveo continued to scrape against the guardrail for several seconds before the assassin also swerved left.

But unlike the Executioner's maneuver, the assassin went too far. The Aveo spun counterclockwise. Tires squealed against pavement as the car went into an uncontrolled spin.

The truck didn't slow.

Bolan slammed his foot on the brake, bringing the Mustang to a screeching halt.

The truck did likewise, but had considerably more momentum on its side, and so did not stop immediately.

Bolan watched as the truck smashed into the Aveo.

2

Lola Maxwell fumed.

It wasn't bad enough that Johnny McAvoy was dead, but they had to send *him* to avenge his death?

No—that was the problem. The man they'd sent had no interest in avenging McAvoy's death. He was just there to finish the job McAvoy had started.

In truth, that was the difference between them. Maxwell honestly couldn't give a damn about bringing Kevin Lee to justice. If it wasn't him selling illegal foreign firearms to the soldiers in the drug trade that ran rampant in south Florida, it would be someone else.

But Lee was the reason her lover was dead—and she intended to kill him for that.

Sleeping with McAvoy had never been part of the plan. Maxwell was a professional, and a professional *never* slept with a partner on an operation.

At least, that was what the rule book said. But the problem with the rule book was that it was hard to find when you were on a long-term deep-cover op.

It wasn't so bad for Maxwell. She was playing the ex-cop hanging out in her old stomping grounds. The only difference was that she was still on the job, just nobody knew it apart from McAvoy and Faraday.

But McAvoy had been all alone out there except for her. He spent his days and nights living a lie, and the only person he could truly confide in, besides a handler he spoke to once a week or so, was Maxwell.

It was four months into the op when it had happened. One of the guys in Lee's employ got his girlfriend knocked up, and they decided to get married. "Donald Kincaid" was trying to ingratiate himself into Lee's world, and going to a bachelor party was definitely a way to endear yourself. So he joined them in barhopping and strip-club attending, working their way up and down Duval Street in a drunken stupor.

Afterward, he stumbled to Maxwell's bungalow at five in the morning. He banged on her door, apparently too drunk to even operate the doorbell properly. She climbed out of bed, slipped into a silk robe and opened the door to see McAvoy, much drunker than he should have been while undercover, babbling on and on about how horrible these men were, the way they treated the other people in the bars and especially the way they treated the strippers. And when management tried to rein them in, one of them pulled his Beretta and shoved the muzzle right in his face.

The group of men had been left alone after that, but McAvoy—who'd been pretending to go along with the macho bullshit up until then—had a hard time with this incident. So he drank more.

The ironic thing was that it worked. Finley, one of Lee's top guys, confided in McAvoy as the party was breaking up that he had been suspicious of him, but seeing him three sheets to the wind with the rest of them proved he was an okay guy.

McAvoy had been crying at this point, and Maxwell took him in her arms, the silk of her robe sliding open to reveal her ample cleavage. McAvoy started kissing her neck and working his way down to that cleavage, and Maxwell found herself completely uninterested in stopping him.

Eventually, they made it back to the bedroom, the bathrobe long since discarded, as were his clothes. Because Maxwell looked the way she did, she could have her pick of men, but because of that, she was extraordinarily picky about whom she chose to sleep with outside the confines of the job.

Of course, this was technically within those confines, but it was hard to argue with McAvoy's hungry need that morning. Or hers, if it came to that, as McAvoy was a most sensitive lover.

Now McAvoy was dead, and she was stuck with this Cooper guy.

For Johnny's sake, she hoped that the rumors had at least some truth to them.

"You keep pacin' like that, you'll wear a hole in the carpet."

She glowered at Jean-Louis when he said that. "Bite me, Jean-Louis."

"You ain't my type," Jean-Louis said with a big grin.

Maxwell couldn't help but grin back at that. Jean-Louis liked his women petite. There were many adjectives that could describe the five-foot-ten Maxwell with her perfect hourglass figure, but "petite" was most definitely not one of them.

She and Faraday had been waiting all night for Cooper to come back with her car. She had changed into sweatpants and a white T-shirt, her breasts straining against the cotton. Maxwell knew that her ample breasts were two of her biggest assets—so to speak—and they had proved very handy in allowing her to get the upper hand over men. It was certainly worth trying with Cooper, maybe giving her the opportunity to get back in his good graces.

She was about to ask Faraday what time it was when she heard the distinctive sound of her pride and joy, the '65 Mustang, pulling into the driveway.

"About goddamn time!" she said as she made a beeline for the front door of her bungalow and all but threw it open. The early-morning sun—it was less than an hour after dawn—blinded her briefly, but she blinked the glare away quickly with the ease of long practice.

She was about to yell at the man for taking so long with her car when her eye caught a few more things to yell at him about. There were skid marks on the passenger-side door, the side-view mirror was missing and one of the headlights was broken. That was just what she could see from the front door.

She couldn't help but notice that Cooper didn't look anywhere near as bad off as her car, which was too bad for him. His being badly injured in a manner commensurate with the damage to the Mustang was the only circumstance under which she was willing to even consider the remotest possibility of starting the process of forgiveness.

But no, the bastard was unscathed, apart from his slightly mussed hair.

"What the *hell* happened to my *car?*" she shrieked.

"The other guy's ride is in much worse shape," was all Bolan would say in reply. He moved past her and went inside.

This just made Maxwell angrier. She followed him in and said, "I can't believe this. What gives you the right to—"

But Bolan had grabbed a piece of paper off the notepad that Maxwell kept on a corkboard near the front door. She generally used it for shopping lists and notes for herself or Faraday. "What's the name and address of the place where you get bodywork done?"

Maxwell blinked. "What?"

The Executioner repeated the question, at which point a confused Lola gave an answer. "Ellis Bodyworks—it's on Avenue G on Fat Deer Key. Every local cop, every county deputy, and every state trooper in the Keys has their car serviced there. Why, you offering to pay to fix it?"

As he wrote that information down, Bolan said, "Yes."

Again, Maxwell found herself brought up short by an answer she wasn't expecting from this man. "Really?"

"I need to make a phone call." He folded the piece of paper and pulled a sat phone out of his jacket pocket. "After that, you can take the Mustang to Ellis and leave it there. Pick it up when they're done, and don't worry about the cost."

Maxwell was impressed. She'd been in this game a long time, and she never knew of any op that had the budget to do car repairs on the level necessary for this. In fact, just in case, she asked, "You do realize that this is a very old car that they don't make new parts for it, right? Just replacing that side-view mirror will be fifty bucks, before labor, and that's the cheapest repair on there."

"It's fine," he said, moving back toward the bedroom. "Excuse me."

He went into her bedroom and closed the door. Confusion receded in Maxwell, the outrage coming back full force. She yanked the door open to see the man entering information into the sat phone.

"This is my bedroom!" This time, Maxwell straightened her back, making sure Cooper got an eyefull of her chest.

He didn't once look below her neck. "I'm aware of this room's function. This call is private. Please close the door."

Maxwell let out a noise that sounded like a pipe bursting. But she did leave the room and closed the door, which was all Bolan cared about.

HE'D BEEN UP ALL NIGHT, making sure the truck crash was contained and dealt with. Brognola had sent a cleanup crew, and also used his contacts in the FBI to get someone from the Monroe County Field Office to take charge of the investigation, making sure that the Executioner's role was kept out of any official reports by the local cops, the Feds, or the National Transportation Safety Bureau, not to mention the company that owned the truck, who'd probably do an investigation of its own.

Complicating matters was the fact that the person in the Aveo didn't have any ID on him, and the credit card and driver's license he'd used with the rental car company belonged to a ninety-three-year-old retired plumber from Hialeah who'd died a week earlier.

Now Bolan needed a good-night's sleep before following up on the only lead he had—the "Delgado" person that Kenny V mentioned during the last phone call of his life—but first he had to contact Brognola.

Once he had been connected to the head of Stony Man, Bolan provided Brognola with the information about Ellis Auto Body.

"We'll take care of it, Striker," Brognola assured him.

"I should've just rented a car," Bolan said. "I know

you said to work with this woman, but I question her professionalism."

"She knows the players, Striker. And her reputation is sterling."

"That's what I heard, too, but all the evidence I've seen doesn't even come close to supporting that reputation, Hal."

"Be that as it may, she's a valuable asset. Without her, you'll have a much harder time of it. And now that Lee knows BATF is on to him, he may circle the wagons and we'll have lost our chance to put him away. Time is of the essence here."

"Fine." Bolan had raised his objection, and Brognola had noted it. There was no point in arguing it further. "Any word on our assassin?"

"Yes, and it's not good," Brognola said. "We've ID'd him as a merc named Ward Dayton. We were only able to get a positive on him because he's in the CIA database."

"As a person of interest or a contractor?"

"The latter, unfortunately. They've used him for wet work on any number of occasions in Cuba, Nicaragua, Chile and a few times in North Africa. In fact, my guy at the Company wasn't exactly pleased that you'd killed him."

"I'm only disappointed that he got himself killed before I could find out why he was doing Kenny Valentino—though I have a pretty good guess." Bolan paused before continuing. "Why is the CIA's Central and South American go-to guy putting bullets in two-bit errand boys for gunrunners?"

"That's a good question, Striker. You need to find the answer, but my guess is that this is the first step in that wagon-circling I was just talking about."

"Valentino had a rep for shooting his mouth off, and unlike Ms. Maxwell's rep, it was one I have little trouble believing he earned, and that's based only on the ninety seconds I saw of him before he bought it. If Lee wants to close ranks, Valentino would almost definitely have been near the top of the list of potential loose ends to tie off."

"What's your next move?" Brognola asked.

"Kenny mentioned a lieutenant of Lee's named Delgado. I'm going to pay him a visit. I'll keep you posted."

3

After getting a few hours' sleep on Maxwell's living-room couch, Bolan went to the kitchen to make himself some coffee. Maxwell was nowhere to be found, which the Executioner found both annoying and a relief. The former because he wanted to ask her about Delgado.

He set the coffeemaker to provide him with a full pot. As it gurgled, he looked out the front window to see that the Mustang was gone. Bolan assumed that Maxwell had taken it to the auto body shop.

Once the coffee had stopped brewing, Bolan poured himself a cup and went back into the living room. Laying out each of his weapons on the coffee table, he carefully and meticulously cleaned each one, inside and out. He had separate cleaning kits for the SIG-Sauer, the Desert Eagle and the RRA rifle.

He cleaned the Desert Eagle first, reassembling it before moving on to the SIG-Sauer. Poor maintenance was a common cause of misfires, and the Executioner's life had been saved more than once by his opponents being too stupid to clean their weaponry properly.

He had just finished cleaning the RRA rifle when he heard a car pull into the driveway, one that didn't have the distinctive purr of the '65 Mustang. Rather it sounded like an Oldsmobile with a muffler problem.

When the noise stopped and the bungalow's door opened, Bolan saw that it was indeed an Olds, one that looked like it was brand-new when disco was born— only about ten years younger than the Mustang, but in considerably worse shape.

"Oh, good, you're up," Maxwell said. She had changed out of the T-shirt and sweats she'd had on earlier, and was now wearing a black tank top and hot pink shorts, as well as the same holster and weapon she'd had when he first arrived. Her breasts were bouncing about in the tank top in a manner that she probably hoped would be as alluring as the white T-shirt she'd worn earlier. But Bolan was just as uninterested now as he was before his nap—he had more important things to occupy his mind.

Looking at the coffee and the disassembled rifle, she added dryly, "Make yourself at home."

"Thanks," Bolan said in a like tone. He grabbed the charging handle and the bolt carrier in order to start re-assembling the rifle. "What do you know about someone named Delgado who works for Lee?" he asked.

"Danny Delgado," Maxwell said without hesitating. "He's Lee's right-hand guy. Every time Lee has a meeting of any kind, Delgado stays behind after it breaks up for last-minute instructions."

Faraday, who'd just come into the room, added, "That's why everybody's got their noses right up Danny's ass."

"Where can I find him?" Bolan asked as he swung the rifle shut, the take-down pin sliding into its proper place.

Maxwell shrugged. "Don't know. I never got that close. I only met the man once or twice. What I know about him's by rep only. Johnny probably knew more. Why?"

"Last night, your pal Kenny V got himself shot in the chest by a freelance assassin who derives most of his income from the CIA."

Maxwell paled. "Kenny's *dead?* Jesus." She shook her head. "Kenny was your classic cockroach—figured he'd survive the goddamn apocalypse. Why'd this assassin take him out?"

"He had a close encounter with a truck on the Overseas Highway before I could ask him. That's why your Mustang was so banged up. Anyhow, when he came into Micky's, Valentino was talking to someone on the phone, and he said to tell Delgado that Lee owed him one now."

"That could be anything," Jean-Louis said. "Hot Lips was always doin' deals for people."

"Maybe." Bolan slid a full clip into place with a satisfying click as he spoke. "But the favor he owed might've been giving up Agent McAvoy, which means Delgado's my next target."

"Fine," Maxwell said, "let me make a phone call."

"To who?" Bolan asked.

"Delgado served with Lee, but he didn't come out of it so good. He stepped on a land mine. He walks with a cane, but his groin didn't do as well as his legs."

"He's impotent?"

Maxwell nodded. "But he still likes to watch, so he spends most of his time at strip clubs. Thing is, he binges—he'll go to one joint every night for two months, then never go in there again, instead moving onto the next one."

"So your phone call will be to someone who knows the location of the current strip club of choice." Bolan deduced.

Lola nodded.

Reaching into the pocket of her shorts, she pulled out a cell phone and entered a number.

"Hey, Vin, it's Lola," she said when the connection was made.

Maxwell had placed a call to Detective Vincenzo Monferato of the Monroe County Sheriff's Office. "Hiya, Lo! How's it hangin'?"

"Not bad. How's Betty?"

"Bitching about the humidity, like usual. She wanted to move to Florida to get away from winter, but she didn't say nothin' about humidity. If she wanted to lose humidity, we shoulda gone to Arizona."

"If you moved to Arizona, she'd complain about the heat. It's her nature."

"Yeah." Monferato sighed. "Anyhow, what're you lookin' for?"

Maxwell pouted. "Now what makes you think I'm looking for something? Maybe I just wanted to say hi."

"Yeah, right. C'mon, Lo, you don't ever call me 'less you want somethin', so spill. Whaddaya need?"

"Just wondering where Danny Delgado gets his rocks off these days."

"Y'know that new joint that opened up where the Hooters used to be?"

"Yeah, Vin, I know all the strip clubs in the Keys," she said sardonically. She knew Hooters had closed— Key West was probably the only location where a Hooters had proved unpopular—but she hadn't noticed what had replaced it.

Monferato laughed. "Yeah, okay. The place is called Hot Keys. They even used the same lettering as the Hooters did. Stupid, right?"

"So that's where Delgado's keeping the nonexistent family jewels?"

"Yup. Every night right at ten, he goes in with two of Lee's goons, orders a tequila and ogles the chicks. Except on Sunday. That's when he stays home and watches whatever's on HBO."

"Okay thanks, Vin. That's another one I owe you."

"I ain't keepin' score, Lo. Take it easy."

Maxwell disconnected the call and looked over at Bolan, who had finished assembling his weaponry. "He's at a place called Hot Keys—or, at least, he will be later. It's on Duval."

"Good. Thanks. I'll head there tonight—alone."

Maxwell put her hands on her hips. "You can't go alone. Look, we're supposed to be working together on this."

"We are. You provided the intel I needed, and now I'm going to put it to good use," he said.

"You won't get anywhere near Delgado. He's got guys to protect him from strangers who try to sidle up to him. I can get you close."

"How? You just told me you didn't know him."

"Yeah, but he knows me. I've got a rep around here, plus he knows Johnny and me were a couple."

Bolan raised an eyebrow. "The same Johnny who they just shot as a BATF agent?"

Frowning, Maxwell said, "That's how I was gonna approach him—tell him I didn't know anything about—"

"Most likely the guys you just mentioned will take you outside and shoot you in the back of the head. You're ex-law-enforcement, and you were sleeping with a BATF agent. You're marked by these people. So your best bet is to stay home where it's safe." Bolan almost added, "And out of my way."

Maxwell looked as if she hadn't thought that through. The Executioner figured she was blinded by her desire for revenge. Yet another reason to keep her at arm's length—let her provide intel, but keep her out of the active mission. She was a liability, one Bolan couldn't afford.

That led to another thought. "Do these guys know you live here?" Bolan asked.

To the Executioner's relief, Maxwell shook her head. "They thought I lived with Johnny."

"Still, it's a small island. Keep an eye out."

Maxwell smiled at that. "I always do."

4

Danny Delgado hated the desert.

He had been born in Albuquerque, New Mexico, and he couldn't get out of there fast enough. His father was a cop, and he'd wanted his son to follow in his footsteps, but the last thing Danny wanted was to spend his life humping a radio car—as his father called it—for thirty years in this arid hellhole.

So he joined the Marines, figured they'd send him somewhere better.

It was fine, at first. He was stationed in Germany, which had real weather, not just the seventh circle of hell.

Then two airplanes crashed into the World Trade Center, another crashed into the Pentagon, and a third crash-landed in Pennsylvania, and suddenly the U.S. was at war. Delgado's unit was transferred to Afghanistan.

More of the goddamn desert.

To add insult to injury, whichever brain-dead soldier wrote up the map of the land mines for the Army got it wrong. Delgado had stepped to the left to avoid what the Army map said was a mine, but in actuality the mine was right where Delgado stepped.

Thank Christ for modern medicine, was all Delgado could say. The medics got his ass to a field hospital in record time, and the docs were able to patch him up enough that he could walk and take a piss.

But he couldn't get it up, even with a truckload of Viagra.

Goddamn desert.

The lieutenant who ran his unit was as straight a straight arrow as you could find, so when Lieutenant Lee visited Delgado in the hospital, he was stunned. "My tour's up," the lieutenant said, "and I got a business deal set up down in Florida. I could use your help."

Delgado was in. His disability pay from the Corps wouldn't be enough to live on, so he needed work, and one thing he knew was guns. He was a rifleman in the Corps, and thanks to growing up with a father who made sure his son knew how to use firearms properly, he'd had the best range scores at his father's gun club for several years running.

It had been great. He and Lee had made a shitload of cash, and best of all, they were in Florida. The tropics beat the crap out of the desert.

And the Florida Keys were filled with strip joints. Even before the land mine, Delgado had never had a relationship that lasted more than a month or two. He got bored too easily. Similarly, after a couple months, each strip joint got dull, as he got tired of seeing the same girls over and over, so he'd move on.

Eventually, of course, he ran out of places, but by then, the first place had had enough turnover in the girls that it was like a new place.

Hot Keys was an especially entertaining venue, because Lee owned a piece of it, so Delgado was given the full VIP treatment. The club had two public stages, one up front near the long mahogany bar, and another in back surrounded by small tables. Behind that back-stage was a doorway covered by a velvet curtain. Go straight through the curtain, and you wind up in a circular room with a couch running all along the wall. For twenty bucks, you got one of the girls to come back there with you, and you could sit on the couch and she'd take off all her clothes and dance for you. You could even touch her legs and arms, but nowhere else.

If you turned right at the curtain, though, there was a staircase to the VIP room, where you would get true privacy. What you got depended on how much you paid. It started at one hundred dollars, where you got the same dance as downstairs, but it went on longer, and you also got a bottle of champagne. More money got you more *entertainment.*

And if you were the right-hand man of the guy who owned forty percent of the business, you got whatever you wanted for free. Intercourse wasn't an option, of course, but Delgado was a connoisseur of oral sex, and he loved to give it. And his own impotence meant that the girls generally didn't complain, since they weren't at risk for pregnancy or disease.

Besides which, Delgado was an excellent tipper.

This night, he'd arrived at the club at his usual hour of ten o'clock, carrying the portfolio that contained whatever he might need for the day, and accompanied by Minaya and Daley. Delgado tried to avoid the usual douche-bag behavior of some guys in these places, and so he always took his girls upstairs. The presence of those douche-bags was why he tended to bring Minaya and Daley along. Sometimes people got in his face. Thanks to those two, they never did so twice.

Delgado always stationed himself at the table closest

to the velvet curtain, as it made the trip to the VIP room quick and easy, plus it proved a good view of the dancers and those patrons busy getting a private dance. But someone was sitting at his table.

As Delgado and the bodyguards entered, one of the bouncers—a large Bahamian guy whose name Delgado couldn't remember—went to talk to the man, who was a well-built older guy with short dark hair.

"Excuse me, sir," the Bahamian said in an accented voice, "but this is the gentleman I told you about. This table is his."

"Yeah?" The guy looked up at Delgado. He seemed pissed at first, and Delgado was about to tell Minaya and Daley to do their thing, but then the guy smiled. "Sure, I'll get up. Always willing to help out a fellow jarhead."

Delgado frowned. "You're in the Corps?"

"Was. Went over the first time we went to the Gulf." Holding out a hand, the guy said, "Name's Mike Burns—used to be a rifleman."

"Really?" Delgado returned the handshake. "Me, too. Went after the Taliban till I stepped on a land mine."

The man winced. "Damn. That's gotta suck." He got up. "Well, here's your table."

Delgado held up a hand. "Nah, sit a spell, Mike—I can call you Mike?"

"Sure. And I can call you?"

"Danny—Danny Delgado. Let me refill that beer for you—'less you want somethin' stronger?"

"I could go for a tequila. Straight up—none of that salt crap."

Delgado grinned. "A man of taste. James?"

Minaya nodded, and went over to the bar to order two tequilas. Delgado sat down next to the ex-marine, placing his portfolio under his chair. Both men were seated with their backs to the wall so they could see the stage.

Delgado knew, of course, that it was perfectly possible that this was a con job of some kind, or that this was some random asshole, or another cop like that McAvoy prick, but if there was a problem, he had Minaya and Daley to deal with it. And if there wasn't a problem, and this Burns guy was who he said he was, Delgado was looking forward to spending time with a fellow traveler. You really couldn't talk about the Corps with anyone *but* a fellow Marine, and the lieutenant— Lee—never wanted to talk about the old days.

THE EXECUTIONER was pleased that his ruse seemed to have worked. Burns was a cover identity from a previous op, one which had never been compromised, so he could use it again with impunity here. If anyone in Lee's organization had the wherewithal to check Corps records, they'd find Burns's name.

Assuming the masquerade even got that far. Bolan was hoping he'd only need to assume the alias for the duration of the evening.

The popular song blaring over the speakers came to an end, and an unseen DJ announced that there were new acts on both the main stage and the bar stage. Bolan didn't bother to register their names, as any woman working here would be using a pseudonym for the stage. These women were paid to be fantasies, and the reality of their actual lives was left in the dressing room.

As the three dancers on the stage in front of them gathered up their outfits and ran off through a velvet-curtained wall, three new women—a blonde, a brunette and a redhead—came out onto the stage, dressed in bikinis or other outfits that were at the minimum place-ment and amount of textile to not violate indecent exposure laws. A new song started, and the women danced. The redhead was enthusiastic, or at least faked it especially well, her smile seeming genuine. Her moves corresponded to the rhythm of the song being played. The brunette was bored, her smile obviously fake and not extending to her eyes, and her movements languid. The blonde seemed to be playing in particular to a pair of crew-cut young men in white T-shirts and shorts who, Bolan guessed, had been tipping her fairly well throughout the night. Certainly the pair of them had already dropped considerable cash on alcohol, given their slurred shouts.

The next several hours passed agonizingly slowly for Bolan. He went through his drink as slowly as he could get away with, not wanting to be impaired. He refused Delgado's offer of a cigarette, but the man himself went through almost a whole pack as the night wore on. No one else in the bar was smoking, but Bolan assumed that the same rules that allowed him free run of the VIP room also allowed Delgado to smoke indoors. The two bodyguards on either side of the table likely curtailed any complaints from the other patrons.

After four songs, the dancers changed again, the guys with the crew cuts shortly thereafter taking the blonde into the back room.

The Executioner had honestly never understood the appeal of such places. After all, if he was hungry, he didn't watch someone cook. True, it could be titillating, and Bolan certainly had a normal heterosexual male's appreciation of the female form, but this sort of objec-tification struck him as pointless.

Bolan listened to Delgado's tales of being in-country. "So we're sitting there, and the lieutenant, he says that he just heard it straight from the general—no way in hell there was a Taliban base in the Adi Ghar caves. That's just a crazy rumor, he says, and we're to discourage anyone else from talkin' about it." Delgado leaned forward. "I swear to Christ, two seconds later one of the privates puts CNN on, and they're reporting that Coalition forces just found a goddamn Taliban base in the goddamn Adi Ghar caves."

Bolan laughed. "That's too funny. Damn reporters."

"Hey, it's not like they got in the way or nothin'. I mean, that was a good catch there, it's just that generals don't know their asses from their elbows." Delgado slugged down the rest of his second tequila, then looked at Minaya. "Get me another one, willya?" He glanced at Bolan, then frowned at how much tequila was left in his glass—still his first. "Damn, Burns, what kind of Marine are you? They don't let you into the Corps 'less you got a cast-iron liver. Keep up!"

With the ease of long practice, Bolan managed to make it look like he was gulping down a huge amount of tequila without actually swallowing it. Then he pretended to develop a coughing fit, leaning away from Delgado and the bodyguards so they couldn't see him use the cough to cover spitting the tequila onto the floor. The club's darkness aided in his deception, as the only bright lights were directed at the two stages.

Deliberately slurring his consonants a bit more, Bolan said, "Woo! That's some good stuff."

After letting out a hearty guffaw, Delgado said to Minaya, "Two more, James."

Minaya nodded, and moved toward the bar.

"So hey, I been tellin' all the tales, here, Mikey." Delgado had switched to "Mikey" without prompting after finishing his first tequila.

Bolan nodded. "Good point there, Danny. Okay, well, see—okay, here's one you just reminded me of. See, there was this one time, I was stationed in Okinawa, and this four-star shows up to give us a talk about— Christ, you know I don't even remember what the hell he was talkin' about."

"Like I said, Mikey, generals don't know their asses from their elbows."

"That's for damn sure. Anyhow, after the talk, General What's His Name invites us all to the O-club for a few drinks. You wanna talk about cast-iron livers—man, this guy had platinum. He was drinkin' down Jack Daniel's after Jack Daniel's after Jack Daniel's. And he's a four-star, so none of us can leave till he does, and he wouldn't leave—just kept buyin' round after round." Bolan pointed a finger at Delgado. "And he was like you, Danny, he paid attention. If you didn't keep up, he started yelling." Bolan lowered his voice and affected a Southern accent. "'I've gone drinking with sailors, son, and they are pantywaists who can't hold their goddamn liquor. Are you a sailor, son?'"

That prompted another guffaw from Delgado. "Yeah, I bet ain't nothin'd make a guy drink up than getting something like that thrown at him."

"Sure there is," Bolan said. "There's bein' an airedale."

He continued the story. "I ain't even got to the best part. See, the next morning, we still had to fall in at 0600, and we didn't even get back to the damn barracks until 0500. The general had gotten on a plane back to Hawaii at 0700, and he probably slept it off in the jet. The rest of us, though, had to act like it was a normal day."

Shaking his head as Minaya came over with the drinks, Delgado said, "I swear to Christ, the generals should just take the enemy drinking. That'd win every war."

"What, gettin' 'em drunk, or borin' the shit outta them with their stories?"

"Both!"

They clanked their glasses at that. Bolan was starting to think that it was time to come up with a way to leave, when the DJ announced the next set of dancers to take the main stage: "The lovely Sheena, the amazing Star and the spectacular Tiffany." The Executioner didn't recognize any of those names, so there was probably a shift change at this hour. Glancing at his watch, he saw that it was midnight, so his guess was probably correct.

At the mention of Star's name, Delgado noticeably brightened. Bolan had a feeling that she was Delgado's current obsession. If so, the excuse to leave was likely to present itself four songs from now.

ERICA MAYES, who went under the stage name "Star" at the Hot Keys Club, was putting herself through the Florida Keys Community College with the money she made dancing. Her mother called it "stripping," but Erica had always preferred the euphemism. Besides, she *did* dance. Sure, she did most of it without her clothes on, but her moves were actual dance steps, and were done to the tune of whatever piece of crap song Omar was playing. Erica was partial to slow jazz, but Miles Davis didn't exactly get the dancers bumping and grinding.

Erica was twenty-two, with coffee-colored skin, doe-brown eyes, dark hair that she kept short in order to keep it manageable and nice curves to her figure. Most of the dancers were model-thin, but Erica actually owned a pair of hips. Her breasts were small and perky. Many women in her line of work would get surgical enhancements to raise her from a B cup to a D or higher, but Erica had no plans to stay in this line of work for very long.

Erica's mother had been disgusted when Erica told her what she'd be doing to pay for college. Never mind that she *had* to pay for it herself, since her mom spent all her money on keeping her bar stocked—which she generally depleted nightly. A short, pale, well-built white woman, she'd fallen in love with a large black man, and had gotten pregnant. Erica had never met her father, as he bailed on Mom the minute the proverbial rabbit died. She couldn't recall ever seeing her mother sober.

Her mom always said Erica was too fat, just because she had those hips. It was ridiculous, since her mom weighed three times what Erica did, but rationality and Erica's mother had parted company some time ago. Perhaps that was one of the reasons she'd taken the job at Hot Keys—none of the men there thought she was too fat.

Lately, though, she hadn't been looking forward to coming to work—not since that Danny guy had started showing up….

While the rules were strict on the floor and in the back room, Erica knew that some of the other girls would do a little more for the customer in the VIP room if he—or sometimes she—paid enough. Once behind the closed door of that room, the owners left it all up to the individuals' discretion. Nobody was punished for turning down a request in the VIP room. This was good, as Erica was only willing to dance and tease. Even upstairs, she only allowed the minimum touching that was required on the floor and in the back room. Erica had been dating her boyfriend for a year now, and she had promised to be faithful to him. To her mind, any kind of contact with another man that was in any way sexual was going over the line. She loved Xavier, and she wanted to marry him after she was done with school.

There was, however, one exception to the club's rule: Danny Delgado.

Erica didn't know the specifics—nor did she care— but if Delgado wanted you in the VIP room, you had to do *everything* he wanted. It had been made clear to Erica that, if she didn't comply, she'd be out on her ass, and no club in the Keys would take her on.

So she always did whatever he wanted.

At the very least, actual sex was out of the question. Delgado had a war wound of some kind, so he was limp-dicked for life. Erica had found that to be a relief.

At least he was a good tipper. The previous night, Delgado had given her as much as she usually made in a week.

But she hadn't told Xavier about him. She couldn't bear to.

So far he'd limited himself to kissing and touching her boobs, but he'd been promising more for a couple of days now.

This night, someone was with him, besides the two redwoods he always came in with, laughing like they were old buddies. Erica hoped that meant he'd be too busy shooting the shit with that guy and wouldn't take her upstairs. She also feared that he would bring his friend along.

After the fourth song ended, she left the stage and

went to the dressing room to put her bikini back on. She debated staying back there, but she knew damn well that she'd get in big trouble if she didn't go right to Delgado's table.

So, after securing the bikini top around her breasts and climbing into the bottoms, she screwed a smile onto her face and went to the table by the velvet curtain.

"How're you and your friend doing?" Erica—or, rather, Star—asked in as solicitous a tone as she could fake.

"Just fine, Star baby. This is my fellow Marine buddy, Mikey Burns."

Burns smiled at her and offered a hand. That right there was more polite than ninety percent of the men who came in here. "Pleasure, ma'am," he said.

Returning the handshake, Star said, "Pleasure's all mine, Mr. Burns." He had a firm grip, she noticed, but didn't overdo it. Very controlled. Given the amount of tequila he'd drunk, that surprised her. Steadiness wasn't a common trait in here among anyone who drank.

Bolan, seeing his cue, rose from his chair. He'd hooked the bait, now it was time to cast the line. "I should let you and the lovely lady get on with whatever it is you'll be doing."

Waving his arm up and down, Delgado said, "Nah, that's fine, Mikey. Stick around."

"Nah, Danny, three's a crowd, know what I'm sayin'? Besides, I know I couldn't hold a candle to you in the charm department." Bolan added a wink for good measure, then reached into his pocket to pull out a piece of paper. Glancing around, he saw a waitress with an empty tray going by. "'Scuse me, ma'am, can I borrow a pen?"

The waitress, who was wearing a bustier, miniskirt,

shoes and nothing else, said, "Sure," and handed him a pen off the tray that was wet from condensation that had dripped off cold glasses and bottles.

Writing down the number of the disposable cell phone he'd gotten that afternoon, Bolan said, "I'm gonna be in the Keys for at least another week or so. Gimme a call, maybe we can talk some more old times."

Taking the proffered piece of paper and handing it to Daley without bothering to look at it, Delgado said, "I'll do that, Mikey. You have yourself a good night."

Nodding, Bolan took his leave. Based on the look on Star's face, he was likely to have a better night than she was.

5

When she bought the bungalow, Lola Maxwell had had a state-of-the-art security system installed. There were security cameras all over the place, and any attempt at a break-in would sound an alarm in the sheriff's office on College Road on the other side of the island. Maxwell had enough friends in that department to guarantee a very quick response.

It was for that reason that she wasn't really concerned about anyone from Kevin Lee's organization breaking into her house. Even if they managed to find out where she lived—unlikely, as the deed to the house actually belonged to Maxwell's long-dead aunt—they wouldn't get far once they got here.

The alarm had two options: silent and loud. The latter was what she normally used, as its main purpose was to scare off potential break-and-enter perps, which, on this island, mostly consisted of drunken revelers doing something stupid that they'd regret—if they didn't forget—in the morning.

But ever since she saw McAvoy's dead body in a parking lot on Stock Island, she'd put it in silent mode. If someone broke into her house, she didn't want them to know it, so they'd still be here when one of her deputy buddies showed up.

The Executioner had come back from his excursion to the strip joint and fallen straight asleep on her couch, smelling of tequila and cigarette smoke. He hadn't said anything about how the night went, which pissed Maxwell off, but there was little she could do about it. Maybe she could use her charm and looks to get him to see reason.

It had always worked before.

With Cooper sleeping soundly on the couch, and Faraday off at the Cutter's Wharf, listening to that aging hippie with the acoustic guitar that he liked so much, Maxwell decided to get some shut-eye of her own. Maybe in the morning, she would be able to get some hard information out of her alleged partner.

After unclipping her Beretta holster and placing it on the nightstand—checking to make sure the safety was on—and kicking off her flip-flops, she reached down and pulled the black tank top over her head, then slid the hot-pink shorts down her legs. Maxwell had never been much for underwear.

She tossed the tank and shorts into the hamper and then yanked out the second drawer of the dresser to figure out which nightgown to wear.

The sexy red one? The see-through green one?

After a moment, she realized that she was trying to find a nightie that would entice Cooper. And she also realized that that was a lost cause.

With a sigh, she threw the drawer shut and opened the one below it. She rummaged through until she found a red flannel shirt, put it on and buttoned the bottom two buttons, then climbed into her bed, sliding between the cotton sheets.

Her thoughts roiled with images of McAvoy, Kevin Lee, Cooper and Kenny V—she simply could *not* fall asleep. She tossed, she turned, she threw the covers off, she pulled the covers back over her, she buttoned her shirt all the way up, she unbuttoned the shirt entirely, she pounded her pillow into submission, she abandoned the pillow—nothing worked.

Mostly the image she couldn't get out of her mind's eye was that of McAvoy lying on the pavement of the dive-shop parking lot, blood pooled under his leg.

So she was wide awake when she heard the intruder.

Instinctively, she reached for her Beretta on the nightstand and hopped out of bed, moving as if to throw the covers off, though they were in fact bunched up on the floor in front of the bed.

She padded toward her bedroom door, thinking it might've been Cooper. Because the alarm was in silent mode, she wouldn't know if it went off until she went into the living room, where the code box was.

Just as she reached for the door, she heard a noise to her left, where the door to the half bath was.

Whirling, she started to aim her Beretta forward, but an elbow collided with her jaw, sending her crashing to the floor, pain exploding in her cheek. She felt a tooth or two loosen.

Forcing herself to focus, she looked up and saw Jiminez, one of Kevin Lee's enforcers.

He was staring down at her, and belatedly Maxwell realized that her flannel shirt was unbuttoned, the sides flapped down toward the floor, leaving her entire naked body exposed. Jiminez's face split into a vicious grin that spoke volumes about his intentions with regard to taking advantage of her nudity.

Jiminez's lust probably saved Maxwell's life, as he wasted precious seconds taking in the view, giving Maxwell a chance to shoot the Beretta, nailing the Cuban right in the gut.

Blood soaked the white T-shirt Jiminez was wearing—only on Key West would a prowler be wearing a white shirt and blue shorts—and one hand moved to his belly to cover where the bullet had penetrated flesh and the wall of his stomach.

"You bitch!" Jiminez cried as he reached down with one massive arm to grab Maxwell's gun arm before she could squeeze off another shot.

Even as he yanked Maxwell to her feet, she realized she should have aimed higher. A gut shot would take forever to be fatal, and until then, the big Cuban would just be pissed off.

One meaty hand wrapped itself around Lola's neck, the other still at his belly. "You even try liftin' that arm, and I'll rip your head off, bitch."

She could see the sweat beading on Jiminez's head. Now it was just a waiting game to see who would die first, her or him.

Then the door flew open to reveal Cooper, his SIG-Sauer drawn and leading the way.

Jiminez whirled her, wrapping his entire left arm around Maxwell and using her as a human shield. "The hell're you?" the man asked, and Maxwell felt his massive arm press against her throat, crushing her windpipe and straining her hyoid bone. Of all the ways she expected to die, being strangled by a gut-shot thug in her own bedroom while only wearing an open flannel shirt and Cooper watching was definitely in the bottom ten of what she had been hoping for.

Rather than answer the Cuban's question, Bolan said, "You're not getting out of here alive."

"That's where you're wrong, *pendejo*. See, me and the lady, we're leavin' right now. She's my health insurance. I get to the hospital and get stitched up, and she don't die."

"Not gonna happen."

"You think you can stop me without killing the bitch?"

"First of all, you came in here with the intent to kill the bitch," Bolan said dryly, "so any promise you make to keep her alive is pretty hollow. Secondly, if you do kill her, you lose the leverage she provides. Not that that's much because, thirdly? I really don't care if she lives or dies."

Maxwell tensed, which just made Jiminez's arm on her neck more painful. It was getting progressively harder to breathe. She knew that Cooper wasn't thrilled with her presence, but to just cast her life away like that? What the hell kind of monster was he?

She felt Jiminez's hot, beer-soaked breath on her ear as he spoke. "So I guess we got us an underpass."

"Impasse is the word you mean," Bolan said, "and no, we don't. One of three things is going to happen. You're either going to eventually lose enough blood that you drop her, and then I shoot you between the eyes. Or you'll try to shoot me with her Beretta, which will probably miss, and then I'll shoot you both."

Jiminez looked down at Maxwell's arm, apparently only just now realizing that he could use her weapon. Then again, he hadn't come with a firearm of any kind, probably to avoid making any noise that would awaken the neighbors. Her shot to his belly killed that notion, but Jiminez's feeble mind never made the jump from that to being able to use her Beretta.

Maxwell couldn't help but think that Lee really needed a better class of thug. She was getting tired of not being able to breathe. Spots were forming in front of her eyes, and she would not let this asshole win.

"What's the third thing?" Jiminez then asked Bolan.

But it was Maxwell who answered as she kicked upward and behind her, catching Jiminez right in the balls. "This."

"Jesus!" Jiminez cried, doubling over and loosening his grip on her neck. As soon as his arm went slack, Maxwell twirled away from him, red flannel flaring outward as she brought up her weapon.

But before she finished turning, Bolan had pulled the trigger of his SIG-Sauer, the 9 mm round drilling through the Cuban's forehead, skull and brain matter. Said brain matter splattered all over Lola's carpeted floor and bedspread, along with a considerable amount of blood.

"Nice kick," Bolan said, putting the safety on his SIG-Sauer and holstering it in the waistband of his pants.

Suddenly self-conscious, Maxwell pulled her flannel shirt over as much of her body as it would cover, an action rendered difficult by the Beretta still in her right hand. "Thank you." She shook her head. "How the hell did he get past the alarm?"

"Easy—I disabled it."

She stared at Bolan. "What? Why?"

"To see if this would happen. I had a feeling that you were compromised, but I knew you wouldn't believe me if I said you were, so I disabled the alarm to let anyone who would attack get in without getting the local cops involved. The less official paperwork, the better."

"He could've killed me!"

Bolan fixed her with an annoyed look. "Of course he

wouldn't have. You were handling him just fine—I didn't intervene until you were in danger."

Maxwell blinked twice. "So—so you were watching the whole time?" She pulled the flannel shirt closer.

Bolan moved toward the door. "Get dressed and pack a bag. We're leaving."

The objection Maxwell was about to raise to that died on her lips. She quickly realized that Jiminez couldn't have been the only one who knew. Hell, he couldn't find his big ass with both hands. No, he only went where Lee told him, which meant that Lee also knew where she lived.

As she went to her dresser, she called out to the Executioner, who had gone back into the living room. "What about Jiminez's body?"

"Leave it. With the alarm off, no break-in was reported, and I assume your neighbors won't think twice if you're gone for several days, yes?"

"Yeah," Maxwell said.

"So the only people who would come in to find the body," Bolan continued, "are Lee's people, and we want them to find the body. When an operation like Lee's hits a snag, the first thing they do is tie off the loose ends. When a loose end refuses to be tied, like you just were, it causes panic, which makes it more likely that they'll make a mistake."

Having buttoned her shirt, she climbed into a pair of cargo pants—she had a feeling she was going to need the extra pockets.

Reentering the bedroom carrying his satchel, Bolan said, "Ready?"

"Give me a minute. Where are we going?"

"We'll find out when we're on the road. We're taking Faraday's junk heap—but he can't know where we are."

Maxwell's eyes went wide. "Jean-Louis! He might be a target, too!"

Bolan had been afraid of this. "We can't—"

She checked her watch. The Cutter's Wharf closed at two, and it was now half past, so he'd be home by now. "Our first stop is Jean-Louis's place. We're not leaving him to die."

The Executioner considered arguing the point, then gave in. Faraday had done his time, and now was working for the good guys, in his own way, and Bolan couldn't let him die if it could be avoided.

Besides, two untied loose ends were better than one.

"Fine, we'll head there, first."

"I'll drive," Maxwell said, heading to the bathroom to pack some toiletries.

6

This was far more than Erica Mayes had bargained for.

Danny Delgado had indeed taken her up to the VIP room, but what he wanted her to do was way beyond what she'd ever been asked to do, or expected to be asked to do.

They entered the VIP room, Delgado's two body-guards standing on either side of the door outside. At Delgado's request, the satellite radio in the room had been set on a light-music channel, and the dulcet tones of some Billy Joel song or other wafted over the speakers, but rather than blare it, as was done downstairs, the music was kept low enough to allow a conversation that didn't need to be shouted at the top of one's lungs.

As with downstairs, there was a table and two chairs, but the chairs were cushioned and much more comfort-able than the cheap wood of the ones on the main floor. Next to the table was a free-standing metal ice bucket containing an open bottle of champagne that was wrapped in a napkin, and two plastic flutes were on the table. According to one of the bouncers, they used to be glass until an irate customer threw one at a dancer, broken glass blinding her in one eye permanently, and opening the club up to a massive lawsuit from said dancer.

"Darlin', I got a favor I need you to do for me," Delgado said after pouring them both some champagne.

"Uh, okay," Erica said tentatively. "I mean, I guess it would depend on what it was."

"What do you make a night here, Star? Thousand?"

"Some nights, yeah. Depends on the tippers." Erica felt sweat bead on her forehead. This was not what she had been expecting.

"You'll get ten thousand if you do me this favor, okay? Ten good days' work."

Erica was able to control her rather extreme reaction to this offer only due to her tenure at Hot Keys providing her with nightly practice in hiding her true emotional state from those observing her. It was difficult, though, and she sipped some champagne to help cover. "What would I have to do?"

"Something really simple. I already talked it over with your boss, and he'll give you the rest of the night off."

Dozens of scenarios flew through Erica's head, and all of them involved a true betrayal of Xavier. Would she have to screw one of his friends? One of his bodyguards?

So it was with a combined sense of relief and dread that she reacted to Delgado's next words. "All you gotta do is go to the Cutter's Wharf on Front Street, pick up a guy and get him to take you home."

If anyone else told her this, Erica would have burst out laughing. But Delgado had pull to get the rules of the club—rules that were backed up by Florida State Law—bent.

"Any guy?"

"No—one in particular." Delgado reached into the portfolio he always carried with him and pulled out an 8x10 of a large, bald, no-necked guy who looked big enough to break Erica in two. Hell, he looked big enough to break either of Delgado's bodyguards in two.

"I don't understand, why do you want me—?"

He put a finger on Erica's lips to quiet her. "Nothing you need to worry about, Star, baby. Just work the same charm you worked on me first time I was here, and he'll be eatin' out of your pretty hand."

Delgado took that pretty hand in his. It felt cold and clammy to Erica, and it was all she could do to keep from yanking it away.

"Look, Erica, all you gotta do is get him to take you home. Once you get him inside, we'll take care of the rest. You won't have to betray Xavier, I promise you that."

A pit opened up in Erica's stomach. So shocked was she by the fact that Delgado knew about Xavier, that it took her a moment to realize that he called her by her given name rather than her stage name. "How did you know about—?"

"Doesn't matter."

Erica thought it goddamn well did matter, but she said nothing for the moment, mostly because she was too busy being scared. How powerful was this man? Could he do something to Xavier if she didn't cooperate? To her mother?

"See," Delgado went on, "we know the big guy goes to the Wharf to wet his whistle when he's so inclined, and we know he's there tonight listening to one of those crapass folk acts. What we don't know is where he lives."

"Can't you just follow him?"

"Tried that. He shakes every tail we put on him, and he ain't listed nowhere. Plus he always takes a different route home. You're his type, and we've seen him go home with chicks like you before."

Erica bristled, but choked back her response. She decided that he meant women of her physical type by "chicks like you" rather than whores.

Which was what she was feeling like right now.

Reaching into the portfolio once again, he took out a big wad of bills. "This is 5K—you get that up front. That's 'cause I trust you, Star, and I know you'll do me this favor. What's more, you do this for me, besides getting the other five thousand, I also promise that you're off the hook with me."

Erica frowned at that. "Huh?"

"What I mean is, whenever I come to Hot Keys, I'll still take you up here, and tip you the same amount, but you won't have to do anything. You can sit and read a book for an hour for all I care."

Delgado had an easy time making that last promise, as he'd been, typically, growing bored with this place, and he only figured to be coming back for another week at most. The perks were great, of course, what with the lieutenant being part owner and all, but he knew he was going to need fresh meat soon.

Besides, Erica was a nice girl. Nice girls didn't belong in places like this. So he'd do what he could to accelerate her ability to quit this place and get on with her life, and also take care of Faraday, all in one shot.

WHEN THE GIRL walked into the Cutter's Wharf, Jean-Louis Faraday realized that his night was finally improving.

He'd been in a funk since McAvoy died. Maxwell had been a mess, and then that Cooper guy decided to show up and wreck her car. Of course, Faraday had loaned Maxwell his old rattletrap. He could manage without wheels for a little while. It meant more walking but, as long as it wasn't raining, the island was a good place to get around on by foot.

Usually, though, he could count on coming to Cutter's and having a good time, listening to good tunes, drinking some fine beer, and maybe finding some nice tail to bring home.

Up until the hot chick walked in, only the beer part had worked out tonight. The usual acoustic act had taken the night off—according to Mick, the bartender, he had the flu and the sore throat was bad enough that he couldn't even talk, much less sing— and the fill-in was just *bad.* He couldn't keep his guitar in tune for more than half a song, he had no range, and he kept butchering the lyrics of the songs he covered.

The lack of good music had an effect on the tail quotient, too. Bad music meant fewer babes. The only women in the bar were curvy voluptuous types, like Lola only with a lot more fat, and Faraday was pretty much repulsed. He liked his women the way he liked his milk: fat free.

He was just about to give up on the evening, when a beautiful skinny girl with coffee-colored skin and great hips came in. Best of all, she made a beeline for the bar. Faraday was sitting at a small round table nearby, so he got a good look at how hot she looked in the tight white T-shirt, which allowed a nice lacy bra to be seen underneath, and a pair of very tight electric blue shorts that exposed fully her amazing legs.

She smiled shyly at him as she slid onto the bar stool, then ordered a rum and Coke from Mick.

Mick looked at Faraday, who nodded in response.

Mick nodded right back, understanding. He'd been coming here long enough that Mick knew what he liked.

When Mick brought her the glass, she reached into the small purse she was carrying, but the bartender held up a hand. "It's on the gentleman," he said in his brogue.

Faraday shook his bald head and chuckled. He was many things, but a gentleman was not one of them. Faraday was born in Miami, and had lived all up and down the state. He was born big, and that pretty much dictated how he lived his life. He played high-school football because he was big. He got odd jobs as a door dragon at parties because he was big. He always got what he wanted from people because he was big.

Then he blew out his knee a week before the state championship. Coach gave him a shitload of painkillers so he could play one final game. The knee never quite healed properly, and Faraday became addicted to the pills. He couldn't play football anymore, and he was hooked on the drugs, so he worked as an enforcer for whoever would hire him.

It was in Key Largo that Lola Maxwell had nailed him, and he dried out in the joint. By the time he did his bit—without ratting on his boss, because you didn't do that—he was clean. He also had had enough of the life. He'd been well paid for his enforcement job, and the drug crew he worked for gave him a nice bonus when he took the charge and kept his mouth shut. Good soldiers were rewarded. Nobody said boo when he said he wasn't coming back to work, either. After all, Florida was well stocked with big men looking for work, who were younger and stronger than Faraday, and had more heart for it.

Since he wasn't drugging anymore, the bonus money

was his to spend. If he needed some extra cash, he'd get a job bouncing or loading crates at one of the many piers and docks up and down the Keys. Plus, he was officially one of Maxwell's confidential informants, and as a CI, he got a regular stipend.

His needs were few, so he always had enough to buy a pretty girl a drink.

This particular pretty girl came over to his table, drink in hand. "Thanks so much, Mr. Gentleman."

He chuckled. "Nothing to it, ma'am. Have a seat."

"I will." She had a certain grace when she sat, and Faraday thought that maybe she was a dancer. He wasn't much for strip joints—he knew too much about how they really worked to ever enjoy himself there—so maybe she was one of the local talent.

She held out a perfectly manicured hand. "I'm Star."

"Really?"

She winced. "I know, I know, blame my parents. My mother's car broke down on the way to the hospital, and my Dad had to help her give birth on the shoulder of the interstate. There was a shooting star when I came out, so that's what they called me. Stupid, right?"

"Not at all," Faraday said, though in fact, he thought it was pretty cheesy. "The governor of Alaska named one of her kids 'Trig' because it was her favorite subject."

She had a musical laugh. Faraday loved throwing out odd bits of trivia at people. For one thing, they never expected it from him, being a big guy and all. That usually translated in people's brains to "dumb." Faraday himself had given in to it, going for football at the expense of his academic career, because that was what he, as a big guy, was supposed to do. Then, when he got hooked on drugs, he had to work to pay for this habit that Coach had forced upon him.

Coach was fired two years later, and then he was arrested for distributing steroids to his students. Faraday didn't know what had happened to the man after that—probably jail, or maybe witness protection in exchange for giving up his supplier—but it was always a regret of his that he hadn't been able to take proper revenge on the old bastard after he got out of stir.

But Faraday was tired of just being the big guy—the thug. Whether as a linebacker or as an enforcer, his job was to knock people down until they couldn't get up. He was sick of that. That was why he was only interested in small women. He had to be gentle with them.

For the next hour or so, Faraday learned that Star was a student working her way through college at Florida State, but she was taking a semester off to "enjoy the Keys."

The only breaks in the conversation came when one of them had to use the rest room, or when a new song started and they both winced at how badly the guy on stage was massacring it.

When he started playing "Me and Julio Down by the Schoolyard," Star got up. "You wanna go someplace? Maybe where they're not raping my childhood? My dad was a huge Simon and Garfunkel fan, and this just hurts."

"Thought you'd never ask," Faraday said with a feral grin. "My place is a nice walk from here."

Star smiled. "Works for me."

THE BREEZE BLEW through Erica Mayes's hair as she walked arm-in-arm down Duval Street with Jean-Louis Faraday. The man was huge—Erica felt like she could fit her entire body in one of his forearms—but he seemed very sweet. She feared for what Delgado was going to do to him.

The yarn she'd spun for him was one of four different backstories she had created for "Star" to tell the customers who wanted to know more about her. The only constant was that she was working her way through college, though it was four different colleges, none of them the community college she was actually attending.

Oh, and in all the stories she had a happy family life. That was a pleasant lie.

She paid very close attention to the route they were taking, and by the time they arrived at the small house that Faraday rented, Erica realized that the walk should have taken half the time—but he'd taken them on a very circuitous route.

No wonder Delgado had needed her.

Once they got inside the small, three-room house— just a kitchenette, living room and bedroom, plus a small bathroom—Erica said, "Can I use your bathroom?"

"Sure," Faraday said as he walked toward the fridge. "You want a beer?"

"Okay." Erica actually hated beer, but she was trying to keep him relaxed.

If only she could do the same for herself.

One of the reasons she'd gone with the version of "Star" who was taking a year off from school was because that had the simplest backstory. Her heart was pounding—which she hoped Faraday chalked up to excitement—and she was afraid that he would see through her deception and strangle her right there.

Hell, he could probably smash her head in with one hand.

Once she closed the door to the bathroom, she turned

on the faucet, and let the water run while she pulled the disposable cell phone that Delgado had given her out of her small purse. The contact list on the phone only had one number on it, and Erica called it. She'd left her Treo at home deliberately. She didn't want any evidence that she'd been here, and that included phone calls from her phone at either Cutter's or here.

"Yeah?" an unfamiliar voice on the other end said.

Stammering, she whispered out the address of the place.

"Got it. Give it ten minutes, then say you have to use the can. Stay there until someone knocks on the bathroom door, all right?"

Erica nodded, then remembered it was a phone call. "All right," she repeated.

After splashing some cold water on her face in the vain hope that it would make her feel better—although it did relax her a little bit—she left the small bathroom and went back out into the living room.

The furnishings could kindly be called Spartan. He had one big couch, and that was it as far as where to sit in the living room.

The man himself was sitting on the couch in question, holding two bottles of an amber beer.

"Have a seat, darlin'," he said, patting the couch cushion next to him with one meaty hand.

The next ten minutes took forever to go by. They made small talk about nothing in particular, and then Faraday leaned in.

"You're very beautiful, Star," he said as his large hand cupped her chin. It felt dangerously close to an attempt to strangle her, but she told herself that that was just because of how big that hand was in relation to her head.

But still, she felt as if she was about to be smothered alive.

Instead, he kissed her.

To her surprise, the kiss was quite pleasant. His tongue probed gently into her mouth. It was the first time she'd kissed a man so deeply since she and Xavier had started dating—aside from Xavier himself, of course. In the VIP lounge, she didn't allow kissing, either.

As the kiss deepened, Faraday's hand moved under her shirt. She tensed, but allowed it. She had to force herself to think about the money.

With the cash Delgado was giving her, she could take the next semester off from dancing, devote all her time to studying, maybe add a few more credits, graduate sooner.

So she let Faraday's hand move up to her bra.

She wrapped her arms around his back—they barely made it—so she could discreetly check her watch in mid-kiss.

Nine minutes.

Close enough for jazz.

She broke off the kiss and gave Faraday an apologetic look.

"Sorry, but that rum and Coke went right through me." She added a shy smile. "I'd rather not be distracted by a full bladder."

Faraday grinned. "Me either."

Getting up from the sofa, Erica went into the bathroom, and waited.

7

The Oldsmobile belonging to Jean-Louis Faraday was approaching its owner's house just behind a white Lexus that had parked in front of it.

As soon as she saw the three men get out of the Lexus, Lola Maxwell swerved the Olds to the left and drove to park on a cross street.

"I assume those three are Lee's muscle?" Bolan asked.

Maxwell nodded. "We're just in time." She killed the ignition, then checked her Beretta to make sure she was locked and loaded. It had a full clip, which she checked, slammed back into place and cocked.

Bolan did likewise with both his SIG-Sauer and his Desert Eagle. After climbing out of the Olds, he placed the SIG in a shoulder holster, with the Desert Eagle staying in his right hand. Three on three were probably even odds, but he didn't know how useful Faraday or Maxwell would be in a firefight, and he assumed that Lee wouldn't send people who *weren't* good in a firefight to instigate one.

All things considered, he preferred his odds with a higher-caliber weapon.

The small house had a front and back door. Two of the men went to the back, with the third approaching the front door.

Bolan pointed at Maxwell, then at the back door.

To his relief, she agreed readily, nodding and moving toward the back with her Beretta at the ready.

The Executioner proceeded to the front door.

The hired guns had already gone inside by the time Bolan reached the door. The front door had been unlocked, but on the way over Maxwell had said that Faraday apparently only locked the door when he went to sleep, and then only if he remembered.

Bolan hoped he lived to regret that decision this night.

Inside, Faraday was finishing his beer, waiting for Star to hurry up in the commode when the door opened.

He kept a Beretta in the end table of the couch, which was on the other side of it from where he was sitting. It was the same model Maxwell had—she'd gotten them both together, actually, since Faraday couldn't get a permit as an ex-con. Maxwell never mentioned that Faraday was armed in her reports to whatever government agency had hired her. Hell, half the time, she didn't mention Faraday at all, except vaguely as a CI.

As soon as Faraday started to slide across the couch, a voice said, "Don't be movin', fat man."

Looking up, he saw two of Lee's muscle guys, Brand and Hawkins, the latter being the one who spoke. Brand was aiming a Smith & Wesson .38 special—an actual, honest-to-God six-shooter, like he was in the goddamn Old West or something—while Hawkins backed up his insult with a Glock 17.

Hoping Star would have the brains to stay in the bathroom, Faraday held up his hands. "It's cool."

Brand spoke, then. "You're a hard man to find, Faraday."

"Yeah, that's what all the girls say," he said with a grin. "You want somethin', or we just gonna stand here flappin' gums all night?"

"Mr. Lee says—"

Whatever message Brand was about to impart from Lee was cut off by the .357 bullet that tore through his abdomen, pulverizing his liver, stomach and half his intestinal tract. Blood exploded out of his belly along with the bullet, which continued through to embed itself deep within Faraday's couch.

Even as Brand fell forward, dead, and Hawkins turned to see what had just happened, Faraday dived for the end table.

The time it would take Bolan to recover from the Desert Eagle's considerable recoil and reaim at Hawkins was enough time for Hawkins to squeeze off a shot of his own. Knowing this, Bolan didn't waste time with the reaiming part, but used the recoil from the Desert Eagle to fall to the floor.

Years of martial arts training made the fall harmless to the Executioner, though he temporarily lost his grip on the Desert Eagle.

Three bullets from Hawkins's .38 whizzed over Bolan's head and splintered the wood of the house's door frame with a crack.

However, Hawkins quickly recovered, now aiming downward at the Executioner.

Before he could pull the trigger, though, Faraday had used Bolan's distraction to yank open the end table drawer, pick up the Beretta, take the safety off and fire a shot at Hawkins.

The bullet tore through the fleshy part of Hawkins's left shoulder.

Unfortunately for him, Hawkins was right handed, and the S&W could easily be fired one-handed, as the goon quickly demonstrated, firing his last three bullets at Faraday.

The first two hit the fat man in center mass, but the third went wild, hitting the bathroom door behind Faraday—going right through the cheap wood.

Three screams filled the small house: one was muffled, coming from the bathroom. The second was Faraday, who fell to the couch as the two slugs buried themselves in his massive chest. Looking down at the pool of blood forming on his shirt, he saw that Hawkins had missed the heart, but he'd still bleed out pretty fast if he didn't get medical help quickly.

The third was Hawkins himself. As the man had taken his last shot, Bolan fired his Desert Eagle at Hawkins's calf.

The .357 round completely destroyed Hawkins's right calf, shattering bone and arteries into a thousand pieces. Only a small strip of flesh kept his foot attached to the rest of his body, and he fell to the floor in agony.

LeRoy Hawkins had thought he knew what pain was from his life of violence.

He was wrong.

He just kept screaming.

Clutching his bleeding belly, Faraday was more concerned about the screaming that was coming from his bathroom. Stumbling clumsily to the door, he saw that the .38 round had cut all the way through the cheap door.

He fumbled with the doorknob, barely managing to open it before collapsing to the floor, his vision swimming.

Bolan got to his feet, saw that Hawkins was still

screaming in agony. He'd bleed out before too long without medical attention.

The Executioner jogged to the bathroom, where a woman's screams had grown louder with Faraday opening the door.

Inside was a petite woman, screaming her lungs out. There were no obvious wounds on her, but the shaving mirror attached to the large mirror on the wall had been shattered—probably by Hawkins's shot that went wide when Bolan shot the man.

Glad that she hadn't been hurt by the stray shot, Bolan grabbed her by the shoulders and shook her gently. "It's all right, Star, it's over."

Bolan had, of course, recognized her immediately from Hot Keys. Getting herself under control, she then also recognized him. "Oh my God. You're—"

"Not who you think I am. Are you okay?"

She quickly nodded.

"Good."

Bolan turned toward the back door, wondering what Maxwell was doing, but not sure he should leave this young woman alone with the injured Faraday for company.

Her presence here likely wasn't a coincidence, but he could deal with that when the situation was under control.

"Wait here," he said with a sharp look at Star, then ran to the back door.

8

Slowly, Maxwell moved alongside the back of Faraday's house, Beretta at the ready, wondering how the hell Lee had gotten onto them.

She had gone to great lengths to conceal her home, and Faraday had gone to greater ones. She knew that he'd been followed going home from Cutter's or any number of other places, but he'd always lost the tail.

So how'd they find him this night?

When she got to the edge of the house, she peered around the corner to see David Favre approaching the back door, which was actually two doors: a thin metal screen door and a thick wooden main door.

Maxwell smiled. This, she was going to enjoy.

Because he shared the same last name as a famous NFL quarterback, everyone had pronounced Favre's last name "Fahrv," like the athlete did. Except David pronounced it the way the name was spelled and also pronounced in the original French: "Fav-ruh."

But the guys all loved football so much that they insisted on "Fahrv." And sometimes they just did it to annoy David who could, it had to be said, be a total dick.

From Maxwell's perspective, though, the worst was

during the birthday party for Danny Delgado that Lee had thrown last year on his yacht. Maxwell had arrived before McAvoy, and Favre thought it'd be cute to grab her ass.

After she slapped his hand, she went to the small bathroom on the boat, only to have Favre force his way into the tiny space with her and try to feel her up.

She kneed him in the balls.

Just as he put his fingers on the handle to the screen door, Maxwell fired a shot right at his hand.

She could've gone for a kill shot, but she wanted him to know who killed him.

The sound of the shot was drowned out by gunfire inside, which meant that Cooper was obviously doing his thing. Her Beretta's round splintered the first two knuckles on Favre's left hand.

Favre cried out in pain, and whirled.

"You! Bitch!"

"That would be me, yes," Maxwell said with a sweet smile. "Don't make me have to knee you in the balls again."

Favre raised his Glock 17 with his right hand, his left hand unconsciously moving to steady his grip, as the Glock was *not* a one-handed weapon.

That motion caused considerable pain, as half of that hand's insides were exposed, and bones shifted into unfamiliar positions that they were never meant to fit into.

Favre's finger squeezed on the trigger anyhow, and a 9 mm round whizzed through the air toward Maxwell. Still flush against the house, she had nowhere to move, so she pressed herself against the wall as best she could.

The bullet tore through her left biceps, skidding across the flesh of her arm like a flat rock across water.

Gritting her teeth against the pain, Maxwell said, "Dammit, Favre, that'll leave a scar!"

She'd pronounced it "Fahrv," just to piss him off.

However, Favre was in too much pain to respond. He was now on his knees, his Glock having fallen to the grassy ground, and he clutched his left wrist with his right hand, as if that would ward off the agony.

Maxwell sauntered up to Favre, trying to ignore the bleeding mess of her left arm that sent white-hot daggers of pain all the way from her wrist to her shoulder.

"You want out of here in one piece, Favre," Maxwell said, again mispronouncing his name, "you tell me how you found out where Jean-Louis and I live."

Sweat was pouring down Favre's face as he stared up at Maxwell in somewhat disbelief.

"Screw off, bitch," he said through clenched teeth.

Maxwell shrugged. "Fine."

She raised her Beretta and fired twice at his groin.

The first bullet cut just below Favre's stomach and torpedoed downward, ripping into his colon.

The second went a bit lower, pulverizing one testicle and continuing to the thigh, nicking the femoral artery.

He'd be dead in a few seconds.

"You were never any good with that anyhow."

"Fuck…you…" The words were a struggle.

"Been wanting to shoot that thing off since Danny's birthday, Favre."

"It's…it's 'Fav-ruh,' you…you…stupid bitch…"

Those were Favre's last words.

Stepping over his corpse, Lola opened the screen door at the same time that someone else opened the inner door.

Throwing the door open the rest of the way, and

ignoring the pain slicing through her left arm, Maxwell raised her Beretta.

On the other side, the Executioner did likewise with his Desert Eagle.

When they each recognized each other, the weapons both lowered.

"Call an ambulance," Bolan said without preamble. "Faraday's been shot."

Tears welled in Maxwell's eyes as she reached into her pocket for her cell—or, rather, tried to with her left hand, but she couldn't raise it high enough to put her hand in her pocket. Holstering the Beretta with her right hand, she then reached across her body to pull out the phone.

"Will he be okay?" she asked.

"Depends on how fast the ambulance you're about to call gets here. He took two shots to the chest."

One-handed, Lola turned on the phone, activated it and then went to the keypad to punch in 9-1-1.

When she was done, Maxwell looked around. Faraday was on the floor at the threshold of the bathroom. If he'd been shot in the chest, it was best not to move him, so she stayed clear until the EMTs showed up.

She just added Faraday to Lee's bill.

A young woman was sitting on the couch, tears having mingled with mascara to make her look like a raccoon. She looked like Faraday's type. The poor kid was probably his booty call for the evening and got stuck with this.

She also saw two corpses: LeRoy Hawkins and Jack Brand. "Damn. The big guns."

"What do you mean?" the Executioner asked.

As she talked, Maxwell went to the kitchenette to clean and bandage her wound. Faraday kept a first-aid kit under the sink. "These two, the guy outside that I iced, and Jiminez—not to mention Pooky, the guy Johnny took down before he died—they're Lee's best guys."

Bolan tilted his head. "So he'll be recruiting?"

She shrugged and winced as she cleaned the wound. "Probably."

The young woman on the couch started crying.

"It's okay, Star," Bolan said. "It's over now."

Maxwell frowned. No way the Executioner would be on a first-name basis with Faraday's squeeze already. "You know her?"

"She's one of the dancers at Hot Keys. She came to Delgado's table right before I left."

Having finished one-handedly wrapping a bandage around her left biceps, Lola quickly moved into the living room, raising her Beretta at Star.

The dancer's eyes grew wide. "What're you doing?" she squeaked.

"Lee owns forty percent of Hot Keys," Maxwell said. "Jean-Louis was *real* careful not to let anyone know where he lived. You're gonna tell me it's a coincidence that the night he takes home someone who works for Lee is the exact same night Lee's people find his house?"

"Put the gun down, Lola," the Executioner said calmly.

"Excuse me?"

"Of course it's not a coincidence. But Star here is a victim, not a villain."

Maxwell was about to object, but then she saw the look of abject fear on the young woman's face. She'd never had a gun pointed at her before, that much was clear. Hell, she looked like she was about to pee in her pants.

She lowered the Beretta.

Bolan looked at Star. "Did they force you?"

Star nodded quickly. "And paid me."

Maxwell rolled her eyes. "That probably made it easier."

"He knew my real name!" Star screamed. "He knew my boyfriend, my mother, where I live…."

"A lot of that going around," Maxwell said.

Bolan rose to his feet. "Can you take care of the local cops?"

Maxwell shrugged. "I guess so, why?"

"Then do that. As far as anyone else is concerned, you came to visit your friend Jean-Louis Faraday, and found him bleeding on the floor, along with three corpses. You don't know what happened. They'll think it's a home invasion gone wrong."

"They'll think it's Lee is what they'll think," Maxwell said with a snort, "once they ID the bodies."

"Whatever." Looking around, Bolan found a pad of paper and a pen hanging from a corkboard on the wall next to the bathroom door. The top sheet had a grocery list. Bolan tore off the sheet under it and wrote down an address on Summerland Key and the same disposable cell phone number he'd given to Danny Delgado. "That's the address of a safehouse. As soon as you're done here, meet us there."

She sighed, holding up her injured arm. "I guess I'll tell them I cut myself shaving. And by the way, how'm I supposed to get there? I assume you're taking Jean-Louis's car?"

Bolan just looked at her and said, "I'm sure you can charm your way into borrowing a car."

With that, he led the stripper out of the house.

Seconds later, Maxwell heard the grinding sound of Faraday's Olds starting up. For her part, Maxwell went out back to retrieve her shell casings. No sense in having shells that would match her weapon floating around.

She heard the sirens just as she got all of her spent bullets pocketed.

9

Erica Mayes had never been so scared in her life.

Seducing Jean-Louis Faraday had been bad enough. That, at least, she could justify with the fact that she'd be getting ten grand at the end of it and her family would be in danger if she didn't.

Now, though, everything had gone to hell, and her mother and Xavier were in awful danger.

Sitting in the passenger seat of the Olds, she stared at the face of the man in the driver's seat, who looked stonily ahead as they drove up the Overseas Highway.

Erica hadn't really gotten a good look at him in the dim lighting of the club, but at Faraday's house, she'd had a much better view.

His eyes. They were ice cold.

As afraid as Erica had been of Delgado, of his bodyguards, of the strange men in the club, of the situation Delgado had put her in, nothing and no one in her life had ever scared her the way the man seated next to her scared her at this moment.

In a small voice, she asked, "Are you going to kill me?"

"Why would I do that?"

The question struck her as ridiculous. "Well, I mean—you killed those other two men."

"They work for a very bad man, Star. It's my job to bring that man and his organization down. You're an innocent victim in all this. I'm not only not going to kill you, I'm going to ask for your help."

Erica swallowed bile. "Why—why would *you* need my help?"

"Delgado put you up to this, correct? Offered you money, threatened your family, as long as you got Faraday to pick you up and bring you home?"

Erica nodded quickly.

"And you were told to stay in the bathroom until it was all over?"

Another nod.

"Good. You're going to spend the night at the safehouse, and then tomorrow you're going to go back to work like usual. When Delgado asks, you tell him that you did as you were told, but when the gunfire stopped, you came out and found a bunch of dead bodies on the floor. You didn't see anything, you don't know what happened, and you ran away scared. Tell them you took this car."

"O-okay. I guess."

"If you don't do what I'm telling you, Star, Delgado will send someone like these men after you."

"They were—" Erica's voice caught. She wiped tears from her eyes and started again. "They were going to take me back home."

"Yeah, well, they're dead—and the house is a crime scene, and will be for a few days at least, so there's not much Lee's people can do that way."

"Maybe I should just go home?"

Bolan shook his head. "I can protect you more easily at the safehouse. Tell them that you drove all night."

"O-okay. I guess." She shivered.

"What's your name?" Bolan asked as the Olds got on the bridge that would take them from Sugarloaf Key to Cudjoe Key. "Your real name," he added.

For a brief instant, Erica debated saying it really was Star, and spinning the same story she had given Faraday, but one look at the man's hard face, and remembering what he did to people he didn't like, she rejected that notion as suicidal. "Erica. Erica Mayes."

"Don't worry, Erica. I'll make sure you stay safe."

A thought occurred to her. "I need to call my mother and my boyfriend."

"That's not a good idea, Erica," Bolan said.

She snapped. "I need to know they're all right!"

"Fine," the Executioner said with the greatest reluctance. He reached into his shirt pocket and handed her the disposable cell phone he'd picked up. "Use this. They may be tracking your phone."

As she took it, Erica said, "My phone's back home. I just have the one Delgado gave me."

"All the more reason not to use it."

Erica called her mother first.

"H'lo?" said a sleepy voice.

"I'm sorry, Mom," Erica said with a wince, "did I wake you?"

"Yes," she said curtly. "Those of us who don't take off our clothes for a living keep *reasonable* hours."

"Sorry, I just wanted to make sure you were okay."

"I'm not an invalid, Erica Jane, I can take care of myself!" her mother said.

But for once Erica didn't mind her mom's attitude. If she was being this obnoxious, it meant everything was normal. For the moment, at least, she was safe.

After ending that call, she called Xavier. As she did

so, Bolan pulled the Olds off the Overseas Highway onto West Shore Drive—only then did she realize they'd arrived at Summerland Key.

Because Erica still lived with her mother, Xavier had his own place on Boca Chica Key, a small studio that barely had room for Xavier's stuff, much less anything of hers, so she only really kept a toothbrush there, as well as half a drawer's worth of clothes. Once she graduated, and got a real job, they'd get their own place together.

Xavier's cell went straight to voice mail, so he was probably home. She then dialed his landline.

A sleepy female voice said, "Hello?"

A pit opened in Erica's stomach. "Who's this?"

"Ashanti. Who's this?"

For a moment, Erica was willing to believe she'd misdialed.

Then she heard Xavier's voice in the background. "Who is it, baby girl?"

"Some chick," Ashanti said.

Erica disconnected.

"Just when I thought this day couldn't get any worse."

Bolan turned right onto a dirt passageway that went about a quarter mile before it reached a tiny house, only slightly bigger than Faraday's place. There was a white Chevy Cavalier already parked there.

After they got out of the car, they were greeted by a tall, lanky, dark-skinned man wearing a blue wind-breaker over the usual Keys ensemble of a T-shirt, shorts, and flip-flops.

"You must be tonight's guests," the man said, reaching into the windbreaker's pocket and flashing an ID. "I was told someone would be taking the house. I'm Agent Fontaine, DEA."

"You guys using this place?" Bolan asked, more than a little suspicious, making a note to himself to have the agent's credentials checked.

Fontaine shook his head. "Nah, I just like comin' here on my days off. I work Miami, and it's just nice to get away from it all. Nobody bothers me here. But I got the call that somebody needed it, so it's back to my crap-ass apartment in Hialeah."

Reaching into the other pocket, Fontaine pulled out a set of keys and headed to the Cavalier.

After the car pulled out, Bolan entered the house, telling Erica to stay outside until he cleared it.

"But a DEA agent was just in there," she pointed out.

"So?" With that, Bolan checked the place, his SIG-Sauer in hand.

To the chilly night air, Erica said, "Thorough son of a bitch, aren't you?"

THE NEXT MORNING, Bolan woke up at dawn, as usual, and did his morning workout. First he did some stretches to limber himself up. Then he ran through some basic martial arts exercises, including some combinations, a few self-defense moves and more stretches.

To his surprise, there was a weight room in the safe-house, so he performed some reps with both hand weights and the barbell. Running wasn't an option, so he followed that with prearranged karate forms, which were called kata. They helped not only to condition the mind and body, but also to perfect assorted karate techniques. He did a series of advanced forms that all began and ended in a standing meditation pose.

The first one he did was the oldest known form, *Sanchin* kata. This sixteen-move form was done entirely in the same three-point stance that Bolan had used when he shot at Ward Dayton in Micky's bar, and with deep breathing on each movement.

Once he was done with *sanchin,* he worked his way through the others. *Gekisai Dai* and *Gekisai Sho,* which were created to train Japanese soldiers for battle in the days before World War II. The Executioner had always considered it ironic that he used a technique originally developed to train the enemies of America. *Tsuki no,* a quick and dirty kata consisting almost entirely of punches. *Sai hà,* which was complex and elegant where *tsuki no* was simple and brutal. *Tensho,* similar to *sanchin* in both stance and heavy use of deep breathing. *Seinchin,* a twenty-seven-move form that combined brutality with elegance.

Finally, he did one of his favorites, *yansu,* the moves of which were very elegant. The kata began fast and furious with an explosion of arm movements, then slowed. In particular was one movement that required a downward block with the palm heel, followed by a very slow bringing up of the arm with a wrist block, then the fingers fanning out into a collarbone strike downward. The wrist block and collarbone strike were both slow and deliberate, a challenge to one's discipline to maintain perfect form. That move was performed four times over the course of the kata's twenty moves.

When he finished the form, a voice said, "That was very pretty."

Turning, Bolan saw a bleary-eyed Erica.

"What was that?" she asked.

"It's a martial arts form called *yansu.* That's Japanese for 'stay pure.'"

"How's that working for you?" she asked with a ragged smile.

"As well as can be expected," Bolan said with a shrug. His purity had been taken away from him when his family was killed. Pure stopped being an option when he chose to devote his life to the pursuit of justice.

There was no need to share that with Erica Mayes, however, who had had enough problems these past twenty-four hours.

Before he could discuss a game plan with her, however, the disposable cell rang. Flipping it open, he said "Yes" in a manner that swallowed the word, so the person on the other end wouldn't be sure of the voice of the person on the other end.

"Is this Mike Burns?"

Bolan instantly recognized the voice of Danny Delgado. Affecting the tone he used as the ex-Marine, he asked, "Danny, that you?"

"Yeah, Mike, it's me. Listen—you doing anything today?"

"Nothing I can't cancel, why?"

"I don't know what kind of business you have down here this week, but— Well, I've got a business opportunity that a man of your background might be good for."

"And what might that be?"

"I'd rather tell you in person, Mike, if you don't mind."

"Uh, sure, I guess. Where are you?"

Danny provided an address on Big Pine Key. "It's a diner that my boss owns. Come around one, I'll buy you lunch, and we'll see about doing business."

"Ah—" Bolan hesitated. "Can you make it one-thirty? That way I won't have to cancel what I got going right now."

"That'd be fine, Mike. See you at half past."

With that, the call ended.

"You have something going on at one?" Erica asked.

Before the Executioner could answer, the voice of Lola Maxwell sounded from the front door. "No, he's just pretending to because it makes his cover more convincing. If you're available exactly when the mark wants you, it's suspicious."

"Exactly." Bolan noted that Maxwell was wearing a loose fitting T-shirt and cargo shorts, along with secure sandals. It was the closest she'd come to practical wear since he'd met her. He also saw that her arm was bandaged less sloppily than she had been able to manage with one hand, which meant someone else had redressed it.

Bolan asked, "How'd it go?"

"Jean-Louis is still in a coma, but they got the bullets out and fixed all the damage. If he comes to, he'll be fine, the docs say."

Maxwell took a deep breath and then went on. "The cops bought the story. They're figuring it was a home invasion. Jean-Louis will play dumb with the cops when he wakes up if he sees them before he sees me. Mind you, the evidence isn't going to match up, but unless they can match the three bullets from your Desert Eagle…"

"They can't."

"Then we're fine." She flopped down on the easy chair in the safehouse's small living room.

"How're you doing?" she asked Erica.

"Crappy, thanks for asking," Erica said dryly.

"Here's the plan," Bolan said. "I'm betting that Delgado's offer is going to be hired muscle, since he has some new vacancies in that department."

"All in a night's work," Maxwell said with a grin.

"I might be able to make him a better offer. Mike Burns's business in the Keys can just as easily be trying to buy some guns."

10

Kevin Lee was not having a good day.

First had come the news that the men he sent to take care of McAvoy's girlfriend and her pet thug had all wound up dead. The thug was comatose in a hospital, and the girlfriend was nowhere to be found.

Now Rico was giving him shit about the deal.

Drug dealers were the best customers in this game, Lee had learned, because they bought in bulk and had money to burn, since in the drug trade, demand always was ahead of supply. It was pretty much impossible *not* to make money as a drug dealer.

So many wanted in on it, of course, that territorial disputes were inevitable. That required firepower.

The problem was, drug dealers were also fickle and had explosive tempers. It was why they needed the guns in the first place, truth be told, because they preferred to settle their disputes with violence instead of talking it out like civilized people.

But it also meant they would change their minds about price on a regular basis. Rico was doing that now, right when the deal was about to go down.

The meeting was taking place in a warehouse on

East Rockland Key. It was where Rico kept his stash of heroin. Lee hadn't been thrilled with having the meet there, but Rico had insisted.

If this hadn't been such a huge deal, with a paycheck in the millions, he probably would've given up and sought out another buyer. But Rico was buying more in one shot than Lee usually sold in six months. He had to get this deal done, which meant putting up with Rico's eccentricities.

So he, along with Nieto and Thorne—the only muscle he had left, until Delgado got him some fresh blood—stood in the warehouse, along with Rico and two of his guys, the equal numbers being a condition of the meet.

Rico was bitching about the rifles.

"You told me you was gettin' me some .50 cals, yo. Now I be findin' out that they's .416s. Wussup with that?"

Lee sighed. "The .416 Barretts are better than the .50 calibers."

"How's that, exactly? Last time I checked, five was bigger than four, you feel me?"

"Yes," Lee said patiently, "but the .416s shoot flatter and faster—and they hit harder."

"Seriously?"

Rico sounded dubious, and Lee really didn't think he would be able to follow a detailed explanation of the ballistics involved.

"Look," Lee said, "if you really really want .50-caliber rifles, I can do that, but the delivery won't be for a week."

"A'ight, fine, I'll take the damn .416s, but they better be tight, you feel me?"

"Feeling" Rico was very low on Lee's list of things to do.

"One more thing," Lee said. "We couldn't get all

two hundred MAC-10s, but we made up for it with the same number of MAC-11s. No extra charge."

Lee didn't bother to point out that he got the MAC-10s and MAC-11s at the same price. Rico would think he was getting a deal.

"That's more like what I want to hear, yo. Let's do this."

Then the door to the warehouse splintered open from the impact of a giant black armored personnel carrier.

Lee ducked for cover before the sound of the wooden door being destroyed even consciously registered in his mind. Hiding behind a wooden crate that was labeled as having fishing supplies, but which probably had a ton of heroin, Lee saw that the APC was a modified VAB— *Véhicule de l'Avant Blindé,* which was French for "Armored Vanguard Vehicle." It had probably been bought secondhand from the French. It was painted black, and stenciled with the letters MCSO, meaning it belonged to the Monroe County Sheriff's Office.

Lee didn't carry weapons—he had people for that. Nieto and Thorne whipped out their handguns. Nieto favored a Para-Ordnance Nite-Tac .45 ACP. Thorne also had a .45, but he went with a Kimber Ultra Refined Carry Pistol II.

Both men wasted little time in opening fire.

The .45 rounds bounced off the APC, which was to be expected, but the fire also kept the deputies and whoever else the sheriff's office had sent along from coming in.

Next to them, Rico and his two thugs whipped out a trio of AK-74s. Lee had given Rico the three Kalashnikovs as samples a month earlier.

As the bullets flew through the air, Lee cursed to himself. There was no way that the local yokels were onto him. Hell, BATF couldn't get to him without his finding out about it, so there was no way the damn sheriff's office was getting anywhere near him.

Rico, though, was another story. Besides, this was *his* warehouse, which meant that some deputy or other had found out where it was and got enough probable cause for a warrant.

This was bad on several levels. For one thing, he risked getting arrested, and being caught associating with a drug dealer in a warehouse full of heroin wasn't exactly the sort of thing that kept your career as an arms dealer under the radar.

For another, the way bullets were flying, he was like as not to get hurt. He'd been shot at enough times in the Middle East that he was more than happy to avoid it as much as possible now, which was why he generally went weaponless. If you were unarmed, people were less likely to shoot at you.

And then there was the simple fact that there was no way, after today, that Rico would be a paying customer. He'd either be arrested or dead.

Lee needed to find another buyer.

Once he got out of the warehouse.

Nieto just kept shooting until his clip ran out of bullets. Most of his shots bounced off the APC, but he was okay with that. As long as he and the rest of them kept shooting, they weren't being shot at.

Then he ducked behind another crate and ejected the clip, which clacked to the floor. Reaching into his jacket pocket, he pulled out another, checked to make sure it was full—it'd be just like him to shove an empty clip in his pocket by mistake—then Nieto shoved it into the .45, cocked it and rose to fire another volley over the crate.

Though it took a little longer, when Thorne did run

out of bullets, he dived for cover, letting the drug dealer and his two goons keep the covering fire going.

RICO GLANCED at the gun dealer and his bodyguards with disgust. Hiding when there's work to be done. Just typical. That was why Rico didn't like dealing with white folks. They tended to hire weak-ass coward types.

But Rico's boys, Po-Boy and Light Bulb, they were tight. They were his best boys. Po-Boy was from New Orleans—that was why he had that nickname—and he'd moved here after Katrina. As for Light Bulb, they called him that because he was always getting ideas. Problem was, they were all stupid ideas, which was why he was still muscle and not management.

Besides, Rico did fine handling management by himself.

They all had their AK-74s on auto and just kept pounding. Rico vowed wasn't no police gonna take his ass down without a fight.

FROM BEHIND THE APC, Hal Diaz held his 5.56 mm Smith & Wesson M&P15T rifle. The helmet he wore was fitted with an earpiece, and the voice of Deputy Sheriff Marquez sounded tinny in it. "Anyone got a shot?"

As soon as the two guys with the .45s stopped firing, Diaz leaned his helmeted head out enough to see the inside of the warehouse past the APC, which was half in, half out of the shattered doorway.

On the right side of the APC as he was, he was mostly clear of fire. The three guys with Kalashnikovs were mainly hitting center and left.

Holding up the rifle and peering through its scope, he saw that he had a clean shot on one of the three guys.

Marquez's query was met entirely with negatives, but then Diaz said, "I've got a shot on the one in the blue shirt."

"Take it," Marquez ordered.

Pausing only long enough to make sure his aim was true, Diaz fired.

The 5.56 mm round cut through the air—which was becoming filled with smoke from all the gunfire—and hit Light Bulb right in center mass, the bullet cutting swiftly through flesh, rib and aorta.

As Light Bulb fell to his death, he lost the ability to aim his AK-74, and he sprayed his fire all over the warehouse.

Most of the bullets that flew freely hit walls or crates or other inanimate objects, some ricocheting to other places.

Seven such bullets riddled Po-Boy's chest, slicing his rib cage, heart, lungs and esophagus to ribbons in an instant.

Another ricochet got Thorne in the back of the head just as he had finished reloading his .45, splintering the back of his skull and severing his spine instantly. The bullet flew out of his mouth and embedded itself in a wooden crate.

Seeing his comrade fall, Nieto got pissed. He and Thorne had been best friends since they were kids growing up in Tampa, and he was *goddamned* if he'd let his boy's death go unanswered.

But he didn't aim at the cops. No, he aimed at Rico. After all, it was *his* boy's shot that took out Thorne. That wasn't right.

For his part, Rico was pissed off, and started screaming as he continued to fire at the cops.

With fewer weapons aimed at them, more of the cops came out from behind the APC to try to get a shot off.

Two of them were hit, one in his Kevlar—which still sent him to the ground on his back—and the other in the arm, which wasn't fatal, but kept him out of the firefight.

Meanwhile, Nieto took aim and let a .45-caliber round fly right at Rico's head.

Unfortunately, he missed, the bullet instead bouncing off the warehouse's corrugated metal wall.

Still screaming, Rico didn't even notice the near miss.

But when his AK-74 ran out of ammo and the Kalashnikov kept dry-clicking—that, he noticed.

"Shit!" he cried as he dived to the floor to get Po-Boy's AK-74, but doing so left Rico open to a shot from Diaz, who fired at his head. The rifle bullet entered right under his ear, shattering his jawbone and pulping his gray matter.

Meanwhile, another cop, Jeff Zbigniew, took aim with his own M&P15T rifle and sent a bullet right into Nieto's temple. The bullet, along with skull fragments, brain matter and sizzling hot flesh, blew out the other temple, and Nieto fell to the ground.

The warehouse was then silent. Diaz and Zbigniew, along with Sergeant Russell, moved in, covering each other. They checked the entire warehouse, but all they found were five dead bodies and a whole lot of bullet-ridden crates.

"Clear!" Russell said, with Diaz and Zbigniew repeating the pronouncement.

Russell looked at his two sharpshooters. "Where's the other one?"

Diaz frowned. "What?"

"We had six guys in here—four Latinos, one black, one white. I only count five bodies—the white guy's missing."

Zbigniew and Diaz both shrugged, and Russell shook his head.

"All right, tear apart these crates. There's another asshole in here, and I want him!"

The search, however, turned up no other bodies, dead or alive. It did, however, turn up a huge amount of uncut heroin, with a street value of close to a billion dollars. It was the biggest drug bust of the year, if not the decade, and Marquez was pleased with the end result.

Except for that missing person.

Diaz then found something: there was a side door, which was unlocked, and it was right behind the crates where the three guys who took cover had all dived.

KEVIN LEE HAD USED that door right after Thorne was killed. There was no percentage in staying, and he knew that Nieto would never cooperate with the police if captured—and he certainly wouldn't if he was killed, though Lee was getting tired of people in his employ meeting their ends—so he felt confident in looking out for himself.

For reasons unknown, the cops had failed to secure the perimeter before taking the door—or if they did, the people on that perimeter had left their posts when the shooting started. One was as likely as the other—the sheriff's office was having manpower shortages of late, and cops also tended to go to the defense of their fellows.

Either way, Lee had been able to take advantage and make his escape. He left the Lincoln Towncar he'd arrived in behind. It was Thorne's anyhow, with no connection to Lee, so he could safely leave it. Once he was far enough away on foot, he'd call for a cab.

And then he'd call Delgado. They needed a new buyer, and *fast*.

11

Erica nearly jumped out of her skin when the disposable cell phone that Delgado had given her rang.

It had only been about fifteen minutes since Lee's right-hand man had called "Mike Burns" with a potential job offer. Obviously Delgado was doing a considerable amount of phone work.

"Hello?" Erica said slowly.

"Star, that you?"

"Oh, God, Danny," Erica said breathlessly, "I'm so scared! I don't know what to do!"

Erica was trying to sound panicky, which wasn't all that much of an effort, all things considered.

"Calm down, Star, baby, it's all right. Tell me what happened."

Slowly, haltingly, Erica told the story exactly as Bolan had instructed her to. Most of it was a true rendering of what had occurred. It veered from the truth only at the very end.

"After I didn't hear anything anymore, I—I opened the bathroom door, and there was Jean-Louis! He was dead! And so were the two guys you sent!"

"Describe them," Delgado said.

"I don't know, they were two dead guys!" She took a deep breath. "One was black, one was white."

"No third person?"

"Not that—not that I saw, no."

"Okay, good. I mean, not good, but good that you're okay. What'd you do, then?"

"I ran! Oh God, Danny, what was I supposed to do? Jean-Louis left the keys to his Olds on a hook by the door, and I just took it and ran. I've been driving all night."

"Where are you now?"

"Key Largo."

The Executioner nodded. That was what she was supposed to say.

They talked for a few more minutes, mostly Erica blubbering and Delgado reassuring her that everything was all right.

Finally, Delgado said, "Look, throw that phone away, okay? And come to work tonight like usual—I'll give you the other 5K."

"But—but I didn't—"

"You did exactly what you were supposed to do, baby. Ain't your fault it went sideways. All right?"

"O-okay."

She pressed the End button, then tossed the phone to the couch.

Maxwell was suddenly there next to her, handing her a mug filled with herb tea. "Here you go."

Grateful, she took the mug, steam rising from it, and held it close to her.

Maxwell's phone rang. "It's Vin," she said after checking the display. She went into the kitchen to take the call.

At Erica's confused look, Bolan said, "One of her contacts in the sheriff's office."

While Maxwell took the call, Erica told Bolan what Delgado had said. As she spoke, Bolan took out his Desert Eagle to clean and reload it.

"If he's going to pay you at the club, then he's probably on the level as far as that goes," Bolan said. "If he wanted to take you out, he wouldn't do it in public. He'd have a private place to pay you off."

Somehow, Erica didn't find that reassuring.

Pocketing her phone, Maxwell came back into the living room, holding a mug of her own.

"Vin was calling to show off," she said with a feral grin. "Apparently, Deputy Marquez just made the biggest drug bust of the decade. They found a ton of H in a warehouse on East Rockland Key. There was a shootout, but all the good guys were just winged. Got five dead bodies, though."

"While I'm thrilled that the Monroe County Sheriff's Office is doing its job, I don't understand—"

"Give me a second, okay?" Maxwell said quickly.

Bolan held up his hands in a "go ahead" gesture, then went back to cleaning his weapon.

"One of the DBs was Rico Pinguino, one of the local drug honchos, and two others were two of his muscle. That's not the interesting part—the interesting part is that the other two corpses were ID'd as Rafael Nieto and José Thorne." She smiled at Bolan. "Remember how we were saying that we took out most of Lee's muscle last night? Well, Nieto and Thorne were about the only ones left. What's more, Vin said there was a sixth person, a white guy, who got away."

Having finished cleaning and reassembling the Desert Eagle, Bolan snapped a clip of ammo into place. "So Lee was doing a deal with a local drug kingpin, and now it's gone south. That means he's going to need a new buyer."

DANNY DELGADO SAT at the table near the door of Niko's Diner. The place was about to go out of business when the lieutenant had bought it. He kept the short-order cook and the busboy, fired everyone else and used it as his personal restaurant. It was a good place to hold meetings, for one thing, as it was out of the way on Big Pine Key, but not so far out of the way that it was hard to get to from Route 1.

And the food didn't suck *too* badly.

Delgado puffed on the first cigarette from his third pack that day. He usually didn't plow through them that fast, but this had been a particularly lousy twenty-four hours. Their six best guys were all in the morgue, and the only thing they knew for sure was that two of them were killed by cops.

And their biggest deal of the year just fell apart.

The lieutenant's yacht was full of guns, and they needed to unload them, and soon. Kevin Lee had even made noises about selling at a discount. They couldn't let them sit on the boat too long. Since September 11, the Coast Guard made regular spot checks of yachts that traveled in the Gulf of Mexico, and while those had lessened in frequency of late, the lieutenant's yacht had been hit more than once by such checks.

And it wasn't like the Coast Guard didn't know who Kevin Lee was. They just couldn't prove he was moving guns. Which was why the "random" checks often hit his boat.

Delgado had made all the phone calls he could, and secured three replacements for their lost manpower. Now he was just waiting for some people to call him back—and for Mike Burns to show up.

Right at one-thirty, the big ex-Marine entered the diner.

Minaya and Daley were at the next booth over, and as soon as the man walked in, they checked him out. Daley started patting him down.

"Want me to strip to my underwear, too?" Bolan asked, putting on his alias's cheeky attitude.

Minaya was holding a FoxHound Pro bug detector and running it up and down Bolan's body. Since Bolan mostly worked alone, there was rarely any need for him to be wearing a wire, so standing for this was hardly an issue. As for the pat-down, he'd—reluctantly—left his SIG-Sauer and Desert Eagle in the car.

He'd already driven Erica home, and instructed Maxwell to stay in the safehouse, a direction he was half-expecting her to ignore. She had driven to the safehouse in a Mini Cooper with Alabama plates. The Executioner had debated for several seconds over whether or not to ask her where she'd gotten it, then decided that it wasn't important.

Once the preliminaries were finished, and Bolan had ordered a grilled cheese sandwich and a glass of water, he said, "So what's this about my special talents?"

Delgado grinned. "Well, you're a Marine. That means you have skills most folks don't have regarding, well, violence."

Bolan laughed. "Yeah, I guess you could say that. Need me to beat somebody up for ya?"

"Anybody I point you at, actually."

Shaking his head, Bolan said, "Wait, you're serious?"

"Of course. You think I dragged your ass out here just to feed you a crappy sandwich?"

"Thanks for the testimonial," Bolan said with a wry grin.

Just then, the short-order cook brought the sandwich and the water. It looked flaccid and greasy, which was about what Bolan had been expecting.

Not bothering to even pick it up, Bolan looked Delgado right in the eye. "What, you wanna hire me for some kinda bouncer gig or something? No offense, Danny, I mean, you're a fellow traveler and all, but that's just a wee bit below my pay grade, know what I'm sayin'?"

"Really?" Delgado reached into his omnipresent portfolio and pulled out a few pieces of paper. "See, I understand you were dishonorably discharged. That ain't the sort of thing that leads to high-paying civvie jobs."

Bolan provided a smile that Delgado probably read as him being amused. In fact, the Executioner was impressed that Delgado went to the trouble of looking up the USMC record for "Michael Burns," which was still available for anyone who'd look. Aaron Kurtzman, Stony Man's computer expert, had created that profile, and Kurtzman did his work well.

Aloud, he said, "Depends on the civvie job you're looking for. To give you a for instance, there's some folks 'round this country who think gettin' yourself dishonorably discharged is a character reference. Especially when you were kicked out for shooting some raghead or other."

Delgado leaned back on the vinyl seat of the diner booth. "Go on." He was now curious as to what, exactly, it was that this Marine did for a living.

"You ever hear tell of a group calls themselves Oklahoma Pride?"

Shaking his head, Delgado said, "Can't say that I have. Why?"

"Well, see, what I do is serve as a kind of broker for folks who need to find things under the radar. In this particular case, Oklahoma Pride needs to get their hands on some equipment."

"What kind of equipment?"

Bolan pulled at the sandwich but did not pick it up. "Look, Danny, this ain't none of your concern. I got a line on what I need, so I can—"

Delgado put a hand forward on the table. "Hang on. The guy I work for—he's a good person to do business with. If you're looking to *do* business."

"What I need's kinda specialized."

Leaning back again, Delgado said, "I'm guessing based on the name of your client and the fact that they consider the reason for your discharge to be a character reference, that they're a bunch of neo-Nazis."

Bolan grinned. "They prefer the term 'racial purists,' but yeah. Me, I don't have a problem with nobody long as he don't worship Allah. But mostly the only color I care about is green."

Delgado smiled. "I'm gonna keep guessing, if you don't mind. I think that these folks have had their Second Amendment rights curtailed, and you're looking to rectify that under the table?"

"Yeah, but like I said, I got a line on what I need."

"What if I make you a better offer?"

Bolan hesitated. "I'm listening."

"My old lieutenant, the one I told you about?"

The Executioner nodded.

"Well, I'm working for him now. And we got us a shipment the buyer of which just had to pull out unexpectedly."

Within an hour, Bolan was in the Olds again, driving back to Route 1. He went north initially, away from Summerland Key, wanting to make sure he wasn't being tailed. Once he was sure, he took a circuitous route around Key Largo before going back south. He got off the Overseas Highway at Big Pine Key and drove around some side streets before returning to the main road and thence to Summerland Key.

To his abject shock, Maxwell was sitting in the living room of the safehouse, reading one of the books that had been left on a bookshelf.

She tossed the paperback aside at his entrance and got to her feet.

"Well?"

"Mike Burns is meeting with Danny Delgado and Kevin Lee tonight at Cow Key Marina on Stock Island to discuss the possible purchase of some weaponry."

Maxwell nodded. "Makes sense. That's a pretty public area—means the meet should stay civil."

"I'm not counting on that. For one thing, the meet's on a back road, near a private dock."

"Figures. When is it?" Maxwell asked.

"Sunset."

Folding her arms over her chest, Maxwell said, "I'm going with you."

Bolan looked at her as if she were insane. "They know who you are, Maxwell. You can't—"

Waving one arm back and forth in front of her face, she said, "I don't mean standing next to you, I mean I should be nearby with my handy-dandy 7.62 mm

WASR-10 rifle, with its just as handy-dandy Pentax Lightseeker XL scope, with which I will be able to see all the action and give you a hand if it goes wrong."

At that, the Executioner hesitated. Having a sniper who knew the terrain would be handy—but he still didn't entirely trust Maxwell.

On the other hand, the meet was in three hours. He doubted he could get any backup from Stony Man on such short notice.

Then a thought occurred to him. "Those items are, I presume, at your residence?"

"You presume incorrectly." Maxwell grinned and blew him a kiss. "They're in the trunk of the Mini Cooper I borrowed from a friend—and don't worry, it's a friend who's not in the game at all. She's a bartender at Cutter's Wharf."

Bolan rolled his eyes. "You went back home to get them, didn't you?"

"There was nobody there, although I could tell that someone had broken in after we left. Christ, they even left Jiminez's body. I thought for sure they'd take it."

"Probably hoping a neighbor would notice the smell and call the cops. If there's an APB put out on you, it might flush you out."

Maxwell snorted. "Anyhow, I got fresh clothes— which are now in that bedroom," she added, pointing at the same room Erica had used the previous night, "some ammo and a few other necessities, then I left. Nobody tailed me, and they weren't watching the house."

"You sure? This operation doesn't strike me as being that sloppy."

"Yeah, but they are shorthanded and having a crisis.

They probably don't have the manpower to do that kind of surveillance work."

"Fine, get out of here, then."

Maxwell frowned. "Excuse me?"

"If you're going to be my backup, I want you in place *now*. Pack some food and a canteen, and bring a jar to pee in."

Maxwell shot him a look. "Um, in case you didn't notice, I'm kinda, y'know—female. Peeing in a jar isn't exactly our thing."

"You'll manage," Bolan said with a total lack of interest. "The point is, I want you ready to go. And if you see anything strange, call me."

With an exaggerated sigh, Maxwell headed toward the bedroom. "Good thing I packed some heavier clothes. It gets kind of breezy on the marina."

Bolan wasn't too concerned about anything happening early, especially since Lee and his people were likely running around like headless chickens after the events of the previous night.

But it got Maxwell out of his hair for a couple of hours, and he couldn't bring himself to complain about that.

So far, things were proceeding better than expected. Once he found out where Lee kept the guns—Maxwell seemed to think they'd be on Lee's yacht, but he needed to know for sure—he could take out Lee and Delgado both, secure the weapons and the mission would be over.

Of course, in Bolan's experience, things were never *quite* that easy....

12

Bolan hadn't heard a word from Maxwell since her departure to set up for the meet, which meant one of two things: she was all set and there were no problems or there was a huge problem, so bad that calling him wasn't possible because she was captured or dead.

Either way, the Executioner's play remained the same—attend the meet in character and learn the location of the guns.

Then make sure those guns never get into the wrong hands and put Lee and Delgado out of business.

Bolan drove in Faraday's Olds to the Overseas Highway. The sun was starting to set, and it painted the sky over the Gulf of Mexico a spectacular panorama of purples and oranges.

Traffic was moving slowly on Route 1, so Bolan had a relatively easy time splitting his focus between the road and the spectacular view. It was a clear day, and what few clouds there were in the sky just added to the landscape of color.

The Executioner didn't often get the chance to simply sit back and enjoy the scenery.

As he went over the bridge from Boca Chica Key to

Stock Island, he saw a man, a woman, and two kids, a boy and a girl, neither of whom was more than ten years old. Presumably two parents with their children, they were standing at the railing of the bridge on the walkway along the shoulder, staring out at the sunset. As he drove slowly by, Bolan noticed the girl was pointing at the water where a dolphin was briefly jumping out of the water before diving back under.

It was good to occasionally be reminded of what it was, exactly, that he was fighting for.

Thus braced, he continued over the bridge and then took a left at Cross Street. Following that to Fifth Avenue, he made a right and continued until he reached the marina.

Delgado's directions had been very specific. Just before Fifth hit the marina, there was a dirt driveway, down which Bolan drove. Three other vehicles were parked at the end of it: a black SUV, a white Lexus, and the same beige Cutlass that he'd parked next to in the diner parking lot earlier that afternoon.

Beyond the three cars were two palm trees, and past them an enclosed dock and a supply shed. Further along, down the coastline, were other docks and sheds and various other constructions continuing out of sight.

The Executioner hoped that Maxwell had taken up position on one of the sheds or docks that were a bit farther down the shore. The effective range of her Kalashnikov knock-off rifle was about a hundred yards—farther if you didn't particularly want to hit anything, but just cause a fuss. None of the docks and sheds were more than twenty feet off the ground, so she could've been as far as the distance of a football field away and still have a clear shot.

Two men had set up a card table and were playing gin rummy. The table was set up about thirty feet in front of the four cars, and as Bolan pulled up, one of them signaled to the three people who were standing in front of the SUV.

Bolan recognized both men at the card table from Micky's the night Kenny V was shot. One, in fact, was the pockmarked Latino who'd signaled Dayton to kill "Hot Lips."

Now Bolan really hoped that Maxwell was in place. If those two kept with their card game, things would be fine, but if they got a look at Bolan's face, the whole thing would go to hell quickly.

One of the people standing by the SUV was Danny Delgado, his portfolio tucked securely under his arm. Next to him was a tall sandy-haired man whose face matched the picture in the file on Kevin Lee that Bolan had read on the laptop on the plane. Bolan didn't recognize the third person, a short African American with thick plastic glasses.

Cutting the ignition to the Olds, Bolan opened the door and slowly climbed out, not wishing to make any sudden moves.

The Executioner couldn't help but notice that everyone present was armed—except for Kevin Lee.

Bolan had come to the meet armed and saw no reason to hide it, so his weapon was quite visible in his shoulder holster as he walked toward Lee, Delgado and the short man.

"So you're Mike Burns, the arms dealer."

Bolan grinned. "Nah, like I told Danny here, I'm just a facilitator. See, some folks need to buy things, and some folks need to sell things. I bring 'em together. You must be Kevin Lee, and you really are an arms dealer."

Bolan offered his hand, and Lee returned the handshake.

Looking down at his holster, Lee asked, "Desert Eagle?"

Bolan nodded. "Mark XIX. Got the kick of a Missouri mule, but it gets the job done."

"I suppose—if you want the job to be to destroy everything in your path." Lee smiled as he said it. "I prefer more elegant weaponry. Blades, I've found, have more poetry to them. Plus, it makes the battle more personal. Guns provide too much distance, and a .357 is just a miniature cannon."

"So, what, you're a sword-and-dagger guy?" Bolan asked.

"Yes, since leaving the Corps, I've started collecting swords, actually. Perhaps someday you can see my collection."

"Not my thing, really. I don't give a rat's ass if the battle's personal or not, long as I win it, know what I mean?" He patted the Desert Eagle. "I figure I stand a much better chance with this than something that ain't nobody used for a couple hundred years."

Lee tilted his head. "To each his own. Mr. Delgado tells me that you have an interest in purchasing some crude weaponry of your own on behalf of a collection of racists."

Holding up his hands, Bolan said, "Hey look, I don't make judgments, okay? Their money's as good as anyone's—and they got plenty of it."

"Really?"

"Why so surprised?"

"I've dealt with the likes of your Oklahoma Pride group, Mr. Burns. They tend to be well-stocked with people who blame their economic difficulties on people with skin darker than theirs rather than their own terminal incompetence. Such people usually do not have the funds to procure mass quantities of firearms."

"Well, if we were just talking about the membership, you'd be absolutely right, Mr. Lee. But see, OP's founder is a fella who owns a whole mess of cattle farms. Through good times and bad, folks always need meat, so he's doin' pretty good for himself."

Lee rubbed his chin. "All right, Mr. Burns, we might be able to do business. I have available ten crates of guns, including two crates of thirty AK-74s per, four crates of twenty MAC-11s per, two crates of fifty police-issue 9 mm Berettas per, and two crates of ten Smith & Wesson M&P15T rifles per. That's two hundred and sixty firearms of assorted kind."

Then Lee named a price.

While the price itself was eminently reasonable, Bolan deliberately guffawed. "You're kidding, right? Guy I was talking to this morning was offering me a full four hundred pieces—including some MAC-10s—for half that price."

"You expect me to believe that?"

Bolan shrugged. "Okay, maybe it was three-quarters. But still—"

"Let me guess—your other offer are weapons that were stolen?"

"Yeah, with the serials burned off."

Lee smiled. "Our weapons are off the grid, Mr. Burns. All of them were targeted for destruction by various law-enforcement agencies, and according to any paper-work you care to dig up, they *have* been destroyed."

"That don't make 'em untraceable."

"True, but nobody's looking for them, either."

Bolan pretended to consider it. "Tell you what—you give me the same price them other folks gave me, and I'll do it." Holding up a hand to stave off Lee's next objection, Bolan said, "And before you try another sales pitch on me, Mr. Lee, I should point out that I'm a gift from God right now. You got ten crates of guns and no buyers, and I'm betting you need to offload 'em sooner rather than later. I ain't in any kind of rush, and if I don't like your terms, I got other sources. You got anyone else willing to bankroll this?"

Lee turned and gave Delgado a nasty look. The Executioner had the feeling that Lee was going to have serious words with the man on the subject of giving too much information away. The advantage of befriending Delgado as a fellow ex-jarhead was that he was more willing to part with vital intel to a friendly face.

Then Lee spoke words that surprised Bolan. "I'm afraid I can't simply agree to this deal myself. I'm only authorized to make the deal at the amount I quoted. I'll need to check before I can say yes to the lower price."

The Executioner was, naturally, too much of a professional to react in any way to this information. Outwardly, all he did was shrug and say, "Fine, like I said, I ain't in a rush. Talk to your people, and we can do this thing when you're ready."

Inwardly, though, Bolan's stomach churned. He'd read every piece of documentation that Stony Man had provided, which included information from sources ranging from the Key West Police and the Monroe County Sheriff's Office all the way up to the FBI and the Bureau of Alcohol, Tobacco, Firearms and Explosives, and none of them mentioned anyone above Kevin Lee.

With a mere three sentences, Lee had changed the game—and the mission—completely.

Suddenly, taking Lee and Delgado out wasn't enough. Now Bolan had to not only find out where the guns were, but also who Lee's boss was.

One of those could be accomplished now, at least.

"Any chance," Bolan asked, "of me getting a peek at the merchandise?"

"Depends," Lee said with a smile. "Any chance of me getting a peek at your cash?"

Bolan chuckled aloud and silently cursed. He'd been hoping they'd at least let him inspect the merchandise, especially if it was on a boat, and therefore relatively easy to secure, but he also couldn't bring himself to be surprised that Lee would be skittish on the subject.

"Fair enough, Mr. Lee. You've got my number. Let me know when we do this right. And hey, Danny?"

"Yeah?" Delgado asked.

"Maybe I'll see you tonight at Hot Keys."

"Maybe," Delgado said neutrally, and with a nervous glance at Lee.

Based on the body language, Lee wasn't thrilled with Delgado's handling of things.

Which was probably why Delgado added, "I'm sure we can get this done, Mike, you watch."

"I don't doubt a thing. I'm sure your boss, whoever he is, knows a good deal when he sees it."

Delgado was about to reply, but Lee cut him off with a stern look.

Then Lee looked at the third man and said, "Let's move out."

The third man signaled to the cardplayers with a quick

whistle. They packed up their cards and folded the table in quick succession while Bolan went back to the Olds.

Just as Bolan opened the door, the pockmarked Latino walked past the Olds.

His eyes went wide, and he pulled out a Glock 17, aiming it right at Bolan's head.

Bolan's hand was on his Desert Eagle, but relative to the Latino, he had the car between them. Before he'd be able to draw the .357 and aim it, the Latino would have the opportunity to pull the trigger twice.

So Bolan stayed in character. "Put that thing down, pal!"

"Martinez," Lee said, "what the hell?"

"This is the asshole who chased after Dayton and knocked him off the road! I seen him in Micky's!"

That got his cohort to take out his own weapon, a 9 mm Glock 19.

Before anything else could happen, a short 7.62 mm round tore into Martinez's pockmarked cheek, destroying the right side of his jaw in an instant, and continuing through to the base of the neck, severing his spinal cord from his brain stem.

For the first time since arriving in Florida, the Executioner was grateful for the presence of Maxwell. The Romanian WASRs—variants on the Russian AK-47s—were not precision weapons, and getting so good a shot took incredible skill—not to mention a certain amount of luck.

The shock of Martinez's death distracted Lee's men long enough for Bolan to unholster his Desert Eagle and fire it at Martinez's fellow rummy player.

The .357 round shattered the man's sternum, shredded his lungs and made goulash of his spine on the way out his back. He fell backward, instantly dead, in a bloody pool on the ground.

As he had at Faraday's house, Bolan used the recoil from the Desert Eagle to aid him in taking cover, falling to the ground behind the Olds.

For their part, Delgado and the man with the glasses both unholstered their own weapons. Delgado was carrying a Heckler & Koch USP handgun, while the other man favored a 9 mm Beretta. Lee took several steps backward to stay protected by his two lieutenants.

Neither of those two weapons were armor-piercing, so the sturdy metal frame of the thirty-year-old car was more than ample protection for Bolan, who was suddenly grateful that Jean-Louis Faraday didn't own a newer car that had more plastic than metal, and was therefore far more fragile.

Most of the rounds either ricocheted harmlessly off the frame of the Olds, or whizzed past it, hitting neither the car nor the Executioner. Both men fired continuously, so for Bolan it was simply a matter of waiting until they both ran out of ammo.

If they were smart, they would have staggered their firing patterns so that one would run out first and reload while the other fired. But from the sounds of it, they were both going all-out at once, despite their target being behind a large piece of metal.

Though their firing pattern showed a lack of forethought, Bolan did notice that one set of shots was coming from a different angle—and that angle became more obtuse with each moment. One of the men was moving slowly around so that the Executioner would be caught in a cross fire.

On the roof of one of the enclosed docks, Maxwell

peered through the Pentax Lightseeker XL scope, waiting for people to stop moving so she could get a decent shot.

She'd been in position for hours. She was cold from the breeze blowing in off the Atlantic Ocean, even with the fleece-lined jacket and thick tights she wore. She was hungry, having eaten all three energy bars she'd brought with her hours ago. She was thirsty, having drained the canteen right after the last energy bar. And she had to pee, because damned if she was going to use the glass jar Bolan had insisted she bring along.

Maxwell could have just sprayed the area with fire to confuse people long enough for Bolan to kill them, but the ammo for this thing was expensive, and she wasn't sure if she'd be able to expense anything on this particular op, given how badly everything had gone.

Besides, Cooper, she knew, could deal with Delgado and that guy with the glasses. There was only one target Maxwell cared about.

Unfortunately, when he'd backed up, he'd moved between the two palm trees, which made it difficult for her to get a proper shot.

"You are *not* leaving this place alive, you son of a bitch," Maxwell muttered. "You killed Johnny, and you must die for that."

Cooper was hiding behind Faraday's car while Delgado and the other guy fired at him. Maxwell figured that the man could take care of himself.

All Lee had to do was move a little and she'd have a clear shot.

Finally, she grew tired of waiting, especially since she was about five seconds from peeing into her tights.

So even as Delgado started to move around to the other side of the Olds to nail Bolan in a cross fire, she took aim at the tree that Lee was hiding behind.

The first shot glanced off the tree, sending bits of palm tree bark shrapnel flying off in all directions.

Instinctively, as Maxwell had hoped would happen, Lee ducked his head. This left him vulnerable, as the palm tree only provided cover while he was standing straight. With his head now poking out from behind the tree, she had a perfect shot at his head.

"This is for Johnny, asshole."

The 7.62 mm round flew through the air. Lee had put his hands up near his head when he ducked, so the bullet hit his right hand first, breaking the metacarpus in two as it cut through, proceeding through to his neck.

To Maxwell's disappointment, Lee's hand had retarded the bullet's momentum enough that the round didn't go all the way through his neck.

That disappointment vanished quickly though, as she saw blood spurt out of Lee's neck.

He tried to scream—searing pain shot through his right hand and his neck—but it only came out as a bloody gurgle.

Maxwell decided that this was better. Through the Pentax, she watched as Lee fell to the ground, his left hand futilely trying to stop the flow of blood from his neck, his eyes bugged out, his mouth struggling to scream, his right hand utterly destroyed.

It took him the better part of a minute to die. Maxwell enjoyed watching every second.

Meanwhile, Delgado had run out of ammo first, followed by the man with the glasses half a second later. Once Bolan heard both the Beretta and the H&K dry firing, he rose, pointed the Desert Eagle at the man with the glasses and pulled the trigger.

Half a second later, the man didn't have a chest. The .357 round had destroyed his entire thoracic region, killing him instantly.

As he did so, Bolan also caught sight of Lee writhing on the ground. He retracted his earlier mental praise of Maxwell, as her thirst for revenge had just cost the Executioner a valuable interrogation.

Bolan had taken out the other man first, as he figured Delgado might still have some value alive.

But the time it took to take the shot, be pissed at Maxwell, and turn around was enough for Delgado to have reloaded.

Both men pointed their handguns at each other. Bolan stared down the muzzle of the H&K while the Desert Eagle was aimed right between Delgado's eyes.

"Dammit, Mike, I thought we were brothers. So much for *semper fi,* huh?"

"That's a Marine saying," Bolan said, using his own clinical tones rather than the more freewheeling speaking pattern of Mike Burns. "A good soldier would never say that."

"Army, huh?" Delgado shook his head. "Figures. Betcha didn't serve in the desert, either."

"You'd be right."

Again, Delgado shook his head. "Well, these past two days have sucked. Who you workin' for, anyhow, Mikey?"

"That was my question for you, Danny."

"I can't tell you that, Mikey."

"Can't or won't?"

"Both. If I could, I wouldn't—but I honestly don't have the first clue. I just worked for the lieutenant. He never told me who it was calling the shots, and I never asked. Chain of command, you know? Only one who dealt with the big boss was the lieutenant." Delgado smiled. "You can ask him, but it looks like that ain't an option."

"So now what?" Bolan asked. "We stand here all night? I may not be a Marine, but I was a rifleman, same as you. We're both good shots, and we both have powerful enough weapons that being a good shot is irrelevant. Do we kill each other?"

"Yeah, well, maybe one of us lives. That land mine in Afghanistan did a lot worse to me than that hand cannon of yours could do if you don't hit the heart or head. I'm used to living with pain."

"Living how? Your boss is dead, your organization is pretty much shattered. You've got nowhere to go and nothing to do. Worse, you're liable for any number of criminal charges, and even if you kill me, that doesn't get the heat off you. For one thing, I'm not working alone. For another, there's a dancer at Hot Keys who can tell a wonderful story about a conspiracy to commit the murder of Jean-Louis Faraday."

Delgado's eyes went wide. "Son of a—" Then he chuckled. "It was you, wasn't it? You nailed Favre, Hawkins and Brand?"

"We did, yes," Bolan said to remind Delgado that he wasn't in this alone.

"Shit."

On the dock roof, Maxwell gritted her teeth. She had a clear shot on Delgado, but, relative to her position, Bolan was right behind him, and standing only a yard or so away. It was pretty likely that any shot she took would go through and through and hit Cooper as well.

So she watched the Mexican standoff and hoped that it ended soon.

"So what'll it be, Danny?" Bolan asked. "We just had a very loud, very impressive shootout. Sooner or later, someone will show up to investigate it. Once that happens, it's over for you. For starters, I'm legally permitted to have this weapon."

Delgado smiled. "Yeah, looks like I'm pretty well fucked, doesn't it?"

His wrist bent, and Bolan assumed he was about to lower his weapon and surrender.

Instead he turned the H&K around and placed the muzzle in his mouth, pulling the trigger. Blood, skull fragments and brain matter flew upward into the air behind Delgado as the bullet tore the top of his head off.

The Executioner sighed. Delgado's behavior wasn't surprising, but it might have been useful to have someone he could hand to BATF alive.

Still, it wasn't a priority, and Delgado didn't have the information Bolan needed.

However, the person who did have that intel was lying dead in his own blood between two palm trees.

Bolan waited for the person responsible for that to make her appearance, and within five minutes, Maxwell arrived, a very big smile on her face. "A job well done, I'd say. Sorry I couldn't help with Danny, but I didn't have a clear shot at—"

She cut herself off when Bolan turned around with a look that could kill.

"What the hell?" she asked. "You're welcome!"

"It was good that you took out Martinez," Bolan said, "but you also killed Kevin Lee."

"Wasn't that kind of the idea?" Maxwell asked in genuine confusion.

"Lee was the only one who could tell us where to find his boss."

"His *what?*" Lola's confusion was only growing.

Bolan let out a long breath.

"Lee's the public face," Bolan explained. "He has a boss. But I can't ask him who it is, now, because you killed him."

"When did you find this out, exactly?"

"About five minutes before everyone started firing."

"And I was supposed to know this, how, exactly? I can't read lips, and you didn't give me a way of listening in. I thought the whole idea here was to take Lee down."

"The idea is to take the organization down. After all, this, the person running things can easily pack up and start over somewhere else, and all this will have been for nothing. You got caught up in your own vendetta and forgot the bigger picture."

Maxwell cursed. She couldn't believe that Lee wasn't the top man. In all the months she and Johnny had been working this case, there was never the slightest hint that there was anyone over Lee.

But then, that was probably the point. And also why the operation was so successful.

"Okay, fine, so we've got more work to do."

"No, 'we' don't," Bolan said harshly. "You've gotten your revenge. For you, this is over."

"Like hell. I want the person who gave the order, not the person who did the deed. I *know* Lee didn't shoot Johnny himself—that was probably Pooky, and he's already dead. I wanted whoever gave Pooky his marching orders. I thought that was Lee, but I was wrong."

"We all were," the Executioner muttered. "We need to check out Lee's yacht."

"It's not in this dock," Maxwell said, having seen it from her vantage point. "The Coast Guard keeps an eye on him as much as they can. I've got a friend over there."

"Fine, call your friend," Bolan said reluctantly, having realized that he was stuck with Maxwell for the time being. He might as well take advantage of her contacts.

While she did so, Bolan went to the Olds and pulled his sat phone out of the glove compartment. He needed Brognola to get a cleanup crew here before someone really did respond to the gunshots. He didn't have time to hand-hold the locals just now.

13

Lee's yacht, according to Maxwell's friend in the Coast Guard, was called *Fidelis,* and it was docked at a marina in Key Largo, all the way on the other end of the Keys.

Bolan figured that it had made sense for Lee to keep the guns as distant from him as possible while still being near enough to retrieve them.

"According to Steve, it just docked there a few hours ago, coming up from the south. That's all they know for sure."

"All right, let's go."

They got into the Olds, driving through all the Keys until they arrived at the northernmost of them, and last one before the mainland, Key Largo.

It didn't take long to find the marina in question, and even less time to find the *Fidelis*.

Of course, it was guarded. From the parking lot, Bolan and Maxwell could see a large bald man with a goatee, earbuds in his ears and a rifle slung over his shoulder.

"You know him?" the Executioner asked.

Maxwell shook her head. "Which can work in our favor."

She had already removed her jacket since coming

down off the dock roof, and now she removed the button-down flannel shirt she'd been wearing under it, revealing a tube top. She then peeled off her tights to reveal a pair of boxer briefs.

Smiling at Bolan, she said, "Give me five minutes."

Even as the much-less-dressed Maxwell jogged down to the marina—her breasts leaping about trying to free themselves from the tube top and almost succeeding—Bolan also got out of the car and took aim with his 5.56 mm RRA Tactical Entry rifle.

He'd give Maxwell a chance, but it would be a very brief one.

THE SENTRY HIMSELF was named Paul Thompson. He had been a star hockey player in high school, and was even entertaining offers from NHL scouts, when he got into a fight with some dude in a bar. How was Paul supposed to know that girl was with him? It wasn't like she was turning Paul away or anything.

In any case, Paul was willing to let bygones be bygones once it was clear that the pretty girl was with the dude, but the dude had other ideas. He followed Paul out the door and whipped out a piece. It was just a cheap Walther PPK, but as the guy tripped over a crack in the sidewalk, he shot Paul's calf near the ankle.

He recovered, but his left ankle was much weaker now. He'd never be able to ice skate again, which meant no hockey.

Hockey had been Paul's life. Since he was four, he wanted to be a hockey player. He only listened to Canadian music, because Canadians liked hockey better than Americans. He made a bunch of playlists on his MP3 player, but the only one he ever actually played was the hockey mix, which was all bands from Canada.

Without being able to play anymore, Paul wasn't sure what to do with himself. Like any good hockey player, he knew how to brawl, so he got work as a bouncer at some of the local clubs, most frequently at O'Sullivan's Bar. That led to more work, mostly watching stuff on the docks that needed watching—not so much from law-abiding citizens, but from the law.

Paul hated guns, since one ruined his life, but this particular job—for some guy down in Key West, who'd hired him through O'Sullivan—required him to be armed. So he'd borrowed a shotgun from a friend. He didn't even know how to use it, but he figured it would intimidate people.

Thank God they let him bring his MP3 player. If he'd had to just stand there all night watching this stupid yacht, he'd have gone crazy.

But as long as he had his hockey mix playing on shuffle, he was cool.

It was right in the middle of a Rush song that he saw the girl.

No, screw that, this was a woman. Some of his bouncer gigs were in strip joints, and Paul hated those because the women in there were all fake. Perfectly made up, surgically enhanced, and not at all like real women.

This, though, this was a real woman. Her curves were all natural.

And Paul could see all of them, since she was just wearing what looked like a two-piece bathing suit—and sneakers. She appeared to be jogging, and Paul swore she looked like Lynda Carter in the old *Wonder Woman*

TV show, just bouncing along. In fact, the only flaw she had was a bandage around her left biceps.

She slowed as she approached Paul, and for that, he pulled out the earbuds. Rush was great, but this was better.

"Hey," Maxwell said breathlessly. "Not used to seeing people on the dock here. I was just going out for a jog."

"Nice night for it," Paul said. "I'm just keeping an eye on this boat for someone."

"That why you've got the big gun?"

"Oh, I got myself a real big gun, sweetheart. And I also have this shotgun."

Somehow, Maxwell managed not to groan. "Really? Well, I wouldn't mind seeing it."

Paul slipped the strap off his shoulder and let the weapon clatter to the wooden deck, then moved to undo his shorts. He never once took his eyes off Maxwell's cleavage.

She laughed. "I meant the shotgun, silly."

Paul blushed. "Oh."

"Though we can talk about looking at the other one, too." She added a feral grin.

He bent to pick up the shotgun from the ground, and for the first time he took his eyes off her.

As soon as he did, she kicked him in the side of the head.

Spots exploded in Paul's eyes as his hands moved up to steady his head, which suddenly started swimming.

Maxwell, meanwhile, snatched up Paul's shotgun, noticing that it wasn't even loaded properly. If she pulled the trigger, it'd blow up in her face. If she had known that, she would have goaded him to shoot her.

That option was off the table, so she aimed the gun at him, hoping he wouldn't goad her to do likewise.

"Get out of here."

Paul struggled to his feet, still clutching his head. "I don't—I don't—"

Maxwell lifted the gun up to her neck, hoping it made her look more threatening. "I said get out of here, hot pants! Or I use this gun to get rid of that gun."

Hesitating only because the shotgun belonged to his buddy, and he was going to be *really* pissed that he'd lost it, Paul finally agreed and ran down the marina toward the parking lot where his car was parked.

He figured he wasn't getting paid enough for this.

Bolan shouldered his rifle and joined Maxwell at the *Fidelis*.

"Nicely done," he said.

"He's probably just some local schmuck they hired to keep an eye on the boat," Maxwell said.

Eager to move on to the next order of business, Bolan said, "Let's see what we've got."

The yacht was beautifully appointed, with all the furnishings either in mahogany or brass.

The first place Bolan went was the cargo hold.

Unfortunately, it was empty.

If the *Fidelis* had come into Key Largo that afternoon, it probably meant that, once everything had gone bad the previous night and that morning, Lee sent it to wherever the cache of merchandise was stored, and then directed the boat itself to Largo.

Maxwell, meanwhile, checked Lee's room, but there was nothing. Just a bed, some clothes and an impressive wet bar. There was no documentation of any kind.

They reunited at the wheel, where they discovered a computerized navigation system. Unfortunately, the logs had been wiped. As far as the computer was concerned, the *Fidelis* had never moved from this spot in its life.

Maxwell looked up at Bolan.

"Okay, boss man, now what?"

Bolan rubbed his eyes with the palm heels of his hands before responding. He was suddenly very tired.

"We head back to the safehouse and get a good night's sleep. We'll figure out our next move in the morning."

14

Bolan slept.

He'd let Maxwell drive back to Summerland Key in the Olds while he retreated to the backseat and used the sat phone to contact Brognola. A Stony Man crew had come in and taken care of the scene of the shootout at Cow Key Marina. Lee, Delgado and their three guns for hire were all declared dead, but the manner of their deaths was classified. The former meant that they were officially deceased so that they would no longer be in the system. Among other things, this meant that Lee and Delgado would no longer receive their veterans' benefits, which would have continued if they were not so declared. And the latter forestalled any official investigation into their deaths.

The only potential issue might be if anyone received insurance benefits from their deaths, but Bolan and Brognola both considered that to be extremely unlikely.

The Executioner told Brognola to have the Coast Guard impound the *Fidelis,* and said that he'd contact the big Fed in the morning to discuss their next move.

Once they'd returned to the safehouse, Maxwell—still in the tube top and boxer briefs, but having kicked off her sneakers—asked if Bolan was interested in a nightcap.

He'd declined, which prompted her to remove the tube top and briefs and ask if he was sure.

"Getting involved with someone you're working with is not the smartest move—it clouds one's judgment," he'd said in reply to her nudity. "I'd have thought that tonight would have driven that home to you, since we'd be in much better shape right now if you weren't so focused on avenging your lover's death."

"First of all," she said, putting her hands on her hips in a manner that made her breasts wiggle provocatively, "I didn't know we needed to keep Lee alive. Second of all, I'm not talking about getting involved, I'm talking about sex. You know, letting off steam? Or can you only do that with the gun in your holster instead of the one in your pants?"

He hadn't bothered to respond verbally to that insult, but instead had retreated wordlessly to the bedroom he'd used the previous night.

A part of him was half-expecting her to follow him in, but apparently she wasn't quite that desperate.

Maxwell might have been amenable to casual sex, but Bolan had to at least like the woman he slept with….

So he slept.

Then suddenly he was up and moving toward his SIG-Sauer before his mind was consciously aware of what was going on. Even as his hand closed around the pistol's stock, he realized that there were footsteps outside the safehouse.

Wearing only briefs, he moved slowly toward the window in his room, which had the blinds drawn.

It was possible, of course, that someone from one of the agencies affiliated with Justice was coming to use the place for his or her own needs, and either was unaware or uncaring of the fact that someone already had use of it. These sorts of things happened in this line of work, and if someone nearby needed a quick bolt-hole, they might not have had the luxury of checking to see if this house was occupied first.

He used the barrel of his SIG-Sauer to separate two of the blinds.

This was definitely not a legitimate use of the safe-house.

There were three of them, moving in formation that indicated military training. They all had AK-74 assault rifles, and they all held them like they knew what they were doing.

Also, they were wearing all black: long-sleeved shirts, thin gloves, pants, work boots, and ball caps. As well, greasepaint covered their faces. Bolan could only see as much as he could because of a nearly full moon.

He thought their formation was a bit eccentric, until the Executioner remembered that there was a motion sensor that turned a light on if a car approached on the road leading to the house. Their movements were intentional and meant to avoid tripping it.

These were professionals.

Bolan had only been alerted to their presence because a lifetime of being a soldier in various and sundry wars, both declared and undeclared, had made him an extremely light sleeper.

He moved to the other window and saw three more men moving in the same manner.

Bolan figured he had maybe fifteen seconds before they reached the front and back doors and another thirty for each team to pick the locks, which were high-end locks, but hardly state-of-the-art, and certainly not insurmountable to a team of pros. The safehouse's security was more due to its secrecy and remote location.

Looking at the door, he saw no light shining under it, meaning that Maxwell had turned the light off in the living room that lay between the two bedrooms. The entry to the front was into the living room, with the back door opening onto the kitchen, which, in turn, was open to the living room.

That meant the best place to make a stand was in the middle of the living room.

All this went through the Executioner's head in the first of the forty-five seconds he figured he had. Since the light was out in the living room, he could open his bedroom door without worry about the changing light through the window alerting the enemy.

It took another six seconds to do that and move across the living room to Maxwell's bedroom and determine that her light was out as well. Three more seconds to open the door quickly—opening it slowly increased the likelihood of squeaking—and move to the side of her bed, where she was asleep under a cotton sheet.

The next four seconds were spent clamping a hand over her mouth, which woke her up and prevented her from making any noise. Once she realized it was him, he pointed to the front of the house and held up three fingers, then to the back and held up three more—that took another four seconds.

She nodded in understanding, threw off the sheet—revealing a still-naked body, save for the bandage on her left arm—and grabbed her Beretta, which took another two seconds.

Five seconds later, they were in the living room. Bolan could hear the sound of something metal being applied to the locks of both doors. By his calculation, they had another twenty seconds before they'd be inside.

The couch—where Bolan's Desert Eagle was—faced the front door. Before grabbing his .357, Bolan pointed at Maxwell and then at the front door.

She nodded and stood in front of the couch. The first thing the three front-door hitters would see was a naked woman pointing a 9 mm pistol at them. It might not make much difference—these guys were pros, and less likely to be distracted—but it couldn't hurt to try, and that extra second of distraction might determine the advantage.

For his part, Bolan put the SIG-Sauer in the rear waistband of his briefs, and pointed the Desert Eagle at the back door while standing in a *sanchin* stance for maximum stability.

Then they waited.

They weren't back to back. The front door was in the center of the living room, while the back door was on the far side of the kitchen. So from where Bolan was standing, Maxwell was about three feet to his left.

The back door opened first, and did so five seconds after the Executioner had estimated. As soon as the tumbler clicked aside to allow the door to open, Bolan squeezed the trigger.

The .357 round caught the outer edge of the door as it swung inward, but that did little to slow it. It did send splinters flying through the air, though.

The bullet continued into the crown of one of the gunners, who was still on his knees from where he had been picking the lock, shredding his ball cap and shearing off the top of his skull. Amazingly, it didn't kill him instantly, as the damage was only to his scalp and skull; his brain was still intact.

Exposed as it was, though, the gunner's brain was unlikely to stay in one piece for long, especially since the impact of the .357 round sent him sprawling onto the rectangular wooden platform that served as a make-shift back porch for the house.

Bolan dived behind the kitchen island while shots from two AK-74s pounded into the safehouse.

Once the gunfire had started, the gunners in front gave up on picking the lock and shot off the doorknob, then the point man kicked the door open.

He caught an eyeful of Maxwell.

Then he caught an eyeful of a 9 mm bullet. Max-well's shot pulped the point man's eyeball and carved a tunnel through his brain.

After squeezing off two more shots, Maxwell turned and jumped to the other side of the couch, using it as cover against the AK-74 rounds flying through the front door.

They had lost the element of surprise, but now it was 2-1 instead of 3-1 in favor of the bad guys. Both Bolan and Maxwell would take it.

Bursts of automatic fire came in through both doors. At the pauses, Bolan fired his Desert Eagle and Maxwell her Beretta, but neither was able to take proper aim.

The leather cushions of the couch were proving resistant to allowing the bullets to make it through, but Maxwell knew that was a temporary situation.

Then she noticed that only one weapon was firing through the front door. Glancing over the couch, she saw the shadow of a form in the window next to the door moving toward the side of the house where Bolan's bedroom was.

She caught Bolan's eye, pointed at herself and then at his bedroom. He nodded, then squeezed off three more shots from his Desert Eagle while she ran into the bedroom.

Moving to the window, she grabbed the string for the blinds and yanked it down in order to raise the blinds.

It revealed one of the gunners moving past the window, which was open, with a screen down to keep out the mosquitoes.

The gunner noticed and whirled to point his AK-74 at Maxwell.

But that motion took half a second, and Maxwell already had the Beretta pointed forward. She drilled four shots into his chest, which sent him stumbling backward. Only then did she realize that the man was wearing Kevlar, and she fell to the floor, AK-74 rounds firing over her head through the now-destroyed window screen.

Then, suddenly, the firing stopped, and the gunner yelled, "Shit!"

Thanking the firearm gods for making Russian guns that jammed easily, Maxwell leaped to her feet and fired two shots at her adversary's leg. The bullet shattered every bone in his right foot and ankle. That kept him still long enough for her to place a single shot to his head, which traveled between his eyes and embedded itself in the center of his brain.

Back in the kitchen, the Executioner saw that he couldn't get a shot at the gunners, hiding as they were behind the house walls, but he did have a clear shot of the small wooden platform. The walls were resistant to even .357 bullets, but the wood wasn't.

So he aimed and fired at the porch, splintering the wood and causing the gunners to temporarily lose their footing.

Using the last shots in his clip, Bolan fired at the heads of the two gunners, which were now both in view.

One shot connected, pulping the hardman's right ear on its way through his skull and brain. The other missed.

The man he hadn't hit recovered faster than Bolan expected, firing blindly into the kitchen before Bolan could pull out his SIG-Sauer. The Executioner dived behind the island again. The base of the island was made of oak, so it would hold up for a while, but there were limits.

And then Bolan remembered something he should have thought of while he and Maxwell had been getting ready for the gunners' entrance: this was a government-run law-enforcement safehouse.

Which meant there was an armory in the living-room closet, located about three feet behind him.

Cursing himself, Bolan reached back and risked exposing his left hand long enough to turn the knob to the closet door.

As bullets riddled the door, the Executioner peered inside to see several pistols and rifles of various kinds— which weren't of much use, especially since they weren't loaded, and the man shooting at him was unlikely to give him time to load them—and a rack filled with M-84 stun grenades, or "flash-bangs."

Snagging one, Bolan yanked out the ring and tossed the grenade to the back door, then curled himself into a ball to protect his eyes and ears as best he could.

Even with his eyes closed and his arms covering his head, Bolan could see the flash through his eyelids, which briefly went bright orange. Accompanying that was a loud explosive noise that made Bolan's ears ring.

When the noise died down, the Executioner heard no gunfire, which he took as an encouraging sign that the

M-84 had not only temporarily incapacitated the gunner at the back door, but also the one at the front as well.

Getting quickly to his feet, he saw both men stood dazed in the entryways to the respective doors.

Bolan fired two shots from his SIG-Sauer, and they both slumped to the floor, seconds later, dead without having a chance to bring their weapons into target acquisition.

Maxwell exited his bedroom, rubbing a finger in one ear while blinking quickly. "You wanna warn a girl next time?"

"I warn you, I warn them," Bolan said a bit loudly, as he was having trouble hearing himself talk.

Maxwell looked at the bodies on the floor, then folded her arms over her exposed breasts. "Why is it when I kill people you yell at me, but when you kill people it's okay?"

"Because we needed Lee alive. These six men are professionals. They would never say who hired them—assuming they even knew."

"Yeah, I know, I was just giving you a hard time," Maxwell said with a wry smile. "So now what?"

"Get dressed. This isn't a safehouse anymore."

"I heard that." She moved across the living room toward her bedroom. "You have a new spot in mind?"

"Not yet."

"I think we both need to be off *everybody's* radar until we know what's going on."

"Agreed. Do you have a place in mind?"

"Yup," Maxwell called out from the bedroom. "And don't worry, nobody knows about it—not even Jean-Louis. Hell, I never even told Johnny about it."

Once he was dressed, Bolan grabbed the Canon EOS 50D digital camera that Maxwell had brought with her and went back into the living room to take pictures of each of the gunmen. Between the greasepaint and the blood, they would probably be tough to ID, but he needed to know who these people were.

Once he shot all six of them from multiple angles, he pulled the memory card and grabbed the sat phone.

Shoving the card into a slot in the phone, he called Brognola.

"Striker? What's going on?" Brognola's speech was slurred, as if Bolan had woken him up.

Quickly, the Executioner filled him in on what had happened. "I've uploaded their photos," he finished.

Now wide awake, Brognola said, "Got them. Aaron's running them through the database." A pause, then, "You have a new place to go?"

"Yes," was all Bolan said.

"Good. I'll call you back as soon as I get a hit on these images."

After disconnecting, Bolan packed the remainder of his items, then headed outside. Maxwell followed him a minute later, wearing a T-shirt, cargo pants and sneakers.

Maxwell headed toward the Olds before realizing that Bolan was moving in the direction of a large black SUV, which she assumed the gunmen had come in.

"Why are we taking that?" she asked.

Bolan opened the door and saw that, as expected, the keys were in the ignition. The hardmen were supposed to be quick in-and-out, and they wanted to be able to get away fast once the hit was over.

"Because that Olds can be connected to both of us at this point. This SUV is probably completely clean. Except—"

Bolan dropped to the ground and crawled under the

vehicle, searching on the undercarriage for a GPS tracker. Sure enough, he found one—a Garmin GPS. Then he frowned. "This isn't good."

"What isn't?"

Yanking the GPS out of its slot, Bolan crawled out from under the SUV.

"This," Bolan said, pointing at the GPS, "is a Garmin VIB 11C."

Maxwell frowned. "Okay, I know about the VIB 11— I've got one in the Mustang, actually, but what's 11C?"

The Executioner shook his head. "It's a variant that they make only for the government. There are only about thirty of those things in the world." He walked back to the SUV. "Whoever hired these people has friends in high places. Or is in high places."

Maxwell cut him off before he could get into the driver's side. "It's easier if I drive—I know where we're going."

Bolan nodded. Besides, if Brognola called back while they were on the road, better if he wasn't driving.

"Well, at least some of it makes sense," Maxwell said as she settled into the driver's seat. "If Lee's boss has the kind of connections that gets a government-exclusive GPS put on his goons' car, it's no wonder BATF couldn't get within ten feet."

Bolan had been thinking much the same thing, but didn't bother to voice so obvious a thought aloud. Besides which, he was too busy trying to determine the last route the SUV took.

Normally, VIB 11Cs were secure, but Bolan knew a password that worked on all of them. "Son of a bitch," he said. "The SUV was last at the north end of Niles Road."

Maxwell frowned. "There's nothing up there except a couple of private docks."

"They must have come in by sea. Forget where you were going to take us. Head up Niles Road. I want to see where this car's been."

Maxwell nodded and took a left onto Route 1, then an immediate right onto Horace Street. That eventually crossed with Niles Road, and she took it north for the next two miles until they got to the end of the road.

Bolan's sat phone buzzed and he put it to his ear. "Talk to me, Hal."

"The search was done faster than I'd expected, but I wanted to double-check it to be sure. All six of those men are freelancers who've done work for the CIA and a few other agencies. I checked, and they all have only one handler in common.

"She's retired now, though," Brognola went on. "Actually, she disappeared. Her name's Yvonne Dessens, and six years ago she fell completely off the grid. I'm trying to track down some more intel on her. Give me five more minutes."

The road they were on was completely dark, illuminated only by the full moon and the SUV's headlights. They were approaching a part of the road that was dimly lit, but which stood out like a beacon on the dark road.

"Will do, Hal," Bolan said, and signed off as Maxwell pulled the SUV onto a small dirt patch near the light source.

There was a single boat tethered to a small dock enclosure, lit by a mounted halogen lamp in the enclosure's wall.

The docked vessel was a motorboat that only sat eight. Bolan saw indentations in the leather of six of the eight seats, with the two rear seats remaining flat and untouched.

Like the *Fidelis,* the motorboat had a state-of-the-art computerized navigation system.

Unlike the *Fidelis,* this one hadn't been wiped.

Just as Bolan called up the coordinates of the boat's previous stop to this one, the sat phone buzzed again.

"Okay, Striker," Brognola said without preamble, "here's what we have. Dessens came up in the 1970s, and she did a great deal of work in North Africa and the Middle East. Later on, she was part of Operation Cyclone, the team that worked on arming the mujahideen in Afghanistan in the early 1980s. After that, she was promoted, and she oversaw most CIA operations in Cuba and the rest of Central America. And then right after 9/11, she disappeared."

Bolan frowned. "If she's hiring mercenaries she used to work with, I'd say she still has a lot of her old connections. That would explain how she was able to nail so many undercovers—even McAvoy, in due course." He let out a breath, then said, "Hal, we're at the boat the mercs used. Its computer is giving a latitude and longitude for its previous stop that's nagging at me."

The Executioner read off the coordinates from the computer.

Silence followed on the phone.

"Hal?"

"I was just verifying something on the computer to make sure I wasn't misremembering. That's about halfway between Key West and the Cuban coast, and it's the location of an old undersea listening post. It used to be nicknamed Castro's Lawn. The post was decommissioned during the Clinton administration, though. We needed to be that close in the old days, but with the improvement in tech over the past couple of decades, we don't need to be so near a hostile power or keep people underwater for so long. It was put in that location because there isn't anything else there."

"Well, there's something there now. Possibly the same thing—you sure it was dismantled?"

"I'm looking at the file now, Striker. There's the decom order, and there's the order for dismantling—but I'm not finding a single record of the base actually being dismantled."

"In that case, Hal, I think we've found our weapons cache—and our arms dealer."

15

Yvonne Dessens hated being woken up early.

The best thing for her about being a free agent, no longer beholden to the U.S. government, was that she could sleep whenever the hell she wanted.

So she was quite displeased when somebody woke her up before she was ready to be up—especially if that somebody was her assistant, Marty Anderson.

Anderson had been her assistant at the CIA, too. It had taken a certain amount of arm-twisting to get him to quit with her.

She'd always had a feeling that the house in the Bahamas was the second biggest reason why he eventually gave in and came along.

It had taken her a few years to get him to stop wearing suits all the time and don light shirts and shorts like everyone else, but he got the hang of it eventually.

He had just walked into her bedroom wearing a white button-down shirt and his usual khaki shorts. Anderson actually was supposed to have done that ten minutes ago, after he got the phone call from Jablonski.

But he was deathly afraid to wake Dessens up before she was ready to be up.

But she needed to know what was going on.

Finally, he entered the room and just looked at her, a thin sheet of cotton covering her body, which was clad only in a pair of panties. Her near nudity was not so much of an issue. The biggest reason why Anderson had said yes and followed his boss out of the CIA was that Dessens had promised that the fantasy he'd had of sex with her would at last come true if he came with her to her new endeavor, so it was nothing he hadn't seen plenty of times before—but she looked so peaceful.

While Dessens was in her fifties, she was still in excellent shape. She'd dyed her hair to keep it the same brown it was when she was younger, and she'd made use of moisturizers and exercise to keep herself looking young and in shape. If not for the worry lines around her mouth, she could easily pass for a woman in her thirties.

And she was still damn gorgeous. That fantasy had been in Anderson's head for a reason, after all. From the moment he'd been hired as her assistant, he'd dreamed of ravishing her spectacular body. At home, before he went to bed, he'd imagine ever-more-absurd scenarios that would end with their intense lovemaking. She knew in general how he felt, even though he'd never said anything, because anybody with two eyes and a working brain would know how he felt. But he'd never had the nerve to act on any of his urges.

To his delight, once they moved to the Bahamas and she started her new business, he finally got that nerve, and they'd reenacted as many of his fantasies as were physically possible.

Anderson sighed, bringing himself back to the present. Unable to put it off any longer, he touched

Dessens's shoulder. Her eyes opened suddenly, and she bolted upright.

"What? What is it?" She blinked. "Jesus Christ, Marty, what—"

"The whole operation's screwed," Anderson said without preamble.

Dessens shook her head. "Once more, with clarity."

Speaking slowly and meticulously—one of Anderson's most valuable assets as an assistant was his ability to collate information and state it clearly and unequivocally for his listener—he filled Dessens in on everything he knew about what was happening with Lee's operation on Key West.

"Is anyone besides Jablonski left alive?" Dessens asked incredulously.

"A few, but they're all scared to death. Delgado had set up a buyer, but neither he nor Lee have been seen since they went to the meet. They've been declared dead, but we can't get a straight answer out of the medical examiner." Anderson held up a hand, cutting off a question from Dessens. "And before you ask, I've tried the usual back channels. Their manner of death is classified, and it's at a level I can't break."

"Damn."

"That's not the worst of it," Anderson said reluctantly.

By this time, Dessens had gotten out of bed and put on a bra, fresh panties and a sundress. "Give it to me, Marty, I can handle it."

"The mercs couldn't pull the trigger on the safehouse."

"Shit!" Dessens stood and rubbed her eyes for a moment. "All right, get the boat ready. We need to secure the cache. If Maxwell and her friend took out Perry's team, then they'll probably be able to figure out where the HQ is. And we'll need muscle. Is Jackson available?"

Anderson shook his head. "He's in Angola."

"Harcourt and Harper?"

"Antarctica."

"Why the hell are they—? Never mind, I don't want to know. Jiminez?"

"We sent him to Lee, remember? He was taken out the other night."

"No, the other Jiminez—Jorge."

"Oh—no, he's in Venezuela, along with Graboski and the guy with the funny nose."

"Simpson." Dessens sighed. "What about Stewart and Van Hise?"

"They were fragged in Mexico last week."

"Green and Collins?"

"They retired. Said their wives were sick of—"

"I don't want to hear it." Dessens let out another long sigh. "We sent Hawkins and Brand to Lee too, right?"

"Yeah. The fat man, Faraday, he took them out."

"Great. So basically we're stuck with—"

"Yeah," Anderson repeated. "All we've got available to us are Raviv and Conlon."

Dessens yawned widely enough that Anderson could see her tonsils, then said, "Get me some coffee, then find whatever dive Raviv and Conlon are hung over in and get them to the marina. We're leaving in half an hour."

Anderson wasn't sure he could *find* Raviv and Conlon in thirty minutes, but he said nothing as he headed to the kitchen. Dessens was pissed enough as it was.

He had set the coffeemaker to start before he'd gone to

the bedroom, and in the long period since then, while he'd hesitated and then explained how thoroughly they were all screwed to Dessens, the coffee was long-since done.

Anderson poured half a mug's worth, then put in three scoops of sugar and stirred it for a minute, then poured in two-percent milk.

It was ready by the time Dessens walked into the kitchen, still bleary-eyed.

For her part, Dessens couldn't believe how quickly everything had gone to hell.

Everything had been going so well, too.

For years, she worked her way up the ladder in the CIA, only to find out that Langley had its very own glass ceiling. Men who screwed up regularly got promoted, while she toiled at the same position for years.

Her big break actually came when a nobody congressman from Texas started taking an interest in Afghanistan, and an operation that was beyond dead in the water suddenly became an important concern. After the mujahideen beat back the Soviets, everyone involved was promoted, including Dessens.

But even then, they stuck her with piddly assignments in Central America. Fidel Castro was getting older, and once the Soviet Union fell, no one gave a damn about overthrowing Communist leaders in Central and South America and replacing them with U.S. friendly dictators. Meanwhile, the men who didn't know their asses from their elbows got to handle the fun stuff in the Middle East.

That was where everything was happening.

The straw that broke her back, though, wasn't the mistreatment, the misogyny, or the fact that she was stuck running ops that hadn't mattered since glasnost.

No, it was the fact that she kept an eye on Afghanistan, and kept writing memos pointing out that the mujahideen should not have been left to their own devices.

Then on September 11, 2001, the Taliban, a group that formed out of the ashes of the mujahideen and who had commandeered the latter's weapons and personnel, attacked the U.S.

Even though she was the only person still in the CIA who had been around for Operation Cyclone, Dessens was not consulted on post-9/11 policy regarding Afghanistan.

So she quit, taking Anderson and a zip drive filled with classified information.

Within six months, she had one of the best gunrunning operations in the southern United States, mostly due to her ability to store the goods in an undersea base that almost nobody knew about, and those who did know of its existence thought it had been dismantled.

It was during a trip to Afghanistan that Dessens had met Lieutenant Kevin Lee. She had been visiting to fulfill a contract to supply American troops with bootleg body armor, since what the U.S. government was supplying was woefully inadequate. Lee expressed an interest in getting into her business after his tour was up, and she felt that a strapping young ex-Marine would be a better front for her gunrunning operation than an ex-CIA woman in her fifties.

She had been impressed—and surprised—when Anderson had come to her with the information that "Don Kincaid" was really a BATF agent named John McAvoy. That intel had been passed on to Lee, who had immediately taken care of things.

Then it all went to hell.

In the past, when she'd found a rat in her organization, she'd had said rat terminated. That, she found, was an excellent way to dissuade law enforcement from doing it again. Losing personnel made them look bad, and also made it hard to recruit replacements.

But not this time.

She had stupidly assumed Lola Maxwell to be just another pretty face. In retrospect, she never should have thought that, since that was the means by which she herself had often been dismissed in the CIA.

Plus, Maxwell had that friend. Dessens still had no clue who the man was, but he was lethal.

When Anderson came back, saying that Raviv and Conlon were getting the boat ready, she said, "We're gonna need to go with the backup site. I get the feeling that Castro's Lawn is about to get too hot."

Anderson nodded as they headed out the door. He locked the house behind them, and then they proceeded to the marina. It would take the four of them about an hour or so to load the ten crates that had originally been earmarked first for Rico Pinguino, and then for Delgado's friend Michael Burns.

Years ago, Dessens had negotiated the purchase of a tract of land in Venezuela, which included several caves. That was her backup location if Castro's Lawn ever became unusable, and she suspected that it was about to become so. Even if it wasn't, she didn't want to take any chances.

Raviv and Conlon were waiting on Dessens's personal yacht, which was the same model as the *Fidelis,* only hers was named *Grant* after her father.

Even more than an untimely wake up, Dessens hated having to work with Raviv and Conlon.

Ira Raviv was born in Israel, but left because he felt the Israeli army was too soft. Raviv's idea of a handgun was a rocket-propelled grenade launcher. It was what he used for what he called "soft work."

Raviv was a devout Jew, also, which Dessens had never quite understood, since he was the least spiritual person she'd ever met—and she'd spent most of her adult life in Washington, D.C., so the competition was pretty fierce. But he wore a yarmulke at all times, and refused to work on the Sabbath or during any high holy days.

He also never shut up. As soon as Dessens and Marty arrived, Raviv stood up and smiled underneath his bushy beard.

"We're all set to go, boss lady. Scuba gear's all loaded and double-checked, and the cargo bay's free and clear and ready for whatever you need. Just tell us what to blow up and when to blow it up, and we'll blow it right up for you, right Steve?"

"Yeah," Steve Conlon said.

By contrast to his partner, Conlon could rarely be motivated to use a word that had more than one syllable—and he preferred those words to only have one consonant. Conlon had been a Navy SEAL, then joined LAPD's SWAT team before moving to New York City and joining an elite drug enforcement NYPD task force.

That task force was shut down suddenly, and Conlon was one of five detectives in the unit who turned in their badges. The reasons were never stated publicly, never put in any reports. The unit simply ceased and five cops were ex-cops.

Conlon hooked up with Raviv in Brooklyn, and they started working together.

At first, Dessens had thought that Conlon didn't talk

much because Raviv wouldn't let him get a word in, but she soon realized that Conlon was taciturn by nature. Teaming with Raviv just gave him a good excuse to be the way he preferred.

Dessens stepped on board and programmed the computer with the coordinates of Castro's Lawn. The computer obligingly plotted a course that would get them there at the best possible speed, given current weather conditions and reported ship and boat activity.

"The plan," Dessens said as she steered the boat out of the marina, "is to remove what we've got in Castro's Lawn, and then, Raviv, you get to have fun."

His eyes widening behind his horn-rimmed glasses, Raviv broke into another grin. "You mean I get to blow up Castro's Lawn? Oh, that's great! I've been wanting to frag that place for years, haven't I, Steve?"

"Yeah."

Dessens waited until they were in international waters before letting the autopilot take over. "Let's get suited up," she said.

The minute they arrived at the coordinates, she wanted to start the dive to get to Castro's Lawn. The sooner this was done, the better.

16

After asking Brognola to once again summon the Coast
Guard to take a boat into custody, Bolan and Maxwell
climbed back into the SUV. Maxwell drove them back
down Niles Road, and then onto Horace before getting
on Route 1 and driving north.

They went through Big Pine Key and over the Seven
Mile Bridge, then through several smaller Keys before
arriving at Upper Matecumbe Key.

Turning left onto Park Road, she made an immediate left down a dirt road that wound among the trees,
before reaching a tiny log cabin.

"Last thing I expected to find here."

Maxwell smiled as she put the SUV into Park.
"That's what I said when Maritza showed it to me. After
she passed away, the cabin wasn't listed among her pos-
sessions. She mailed me the deed about a week before
she died, and said I could have the place."

"Who was Maritza?" Bolan asked as he climbed out
of the car.

"Someone who helped me, once."

That had been a bad time in Maxwell's life, and she
wasn't really in the mood to talk about it—especially
not with Bolan. "Come on."

She walked toward the front door, which opened at the slightest push.

Inside was a single room with no furnishings, save for a deflated queen-size air mattress, with a thick quilt folded next to it, piled on top of four pillows.

All were covered in dust.

"I haven't been here for a while," Maxwell said sheepishly.

"It's fine," Bolan said. He'd slept in worse places in his time. "You can have the mattress."

Maxwell rolled her eyes. "Oh for crying out loud, I'm not going to try to molest you in your sleep, all right? If nothing else, I'm exhausted. Trust me, I won't make a single solitary move on you, okay?"

Without waiting for a response, Maxwell got on her knees and activated the pump for the air mattress. Once it was done, she grabbed the quilt and spread it out over the temporary bed, then put two pillows each on either side of the mattress and flopped down on two of them.

"Good night," she said, and closed her eyes.

Bolan wasn't sure whether to be impressed or disappointed that she didn't do a strip tease before going to sleep.

Then again, the last two times she'd gone to sleep in a state of undress, she was almost killed. Perhaps she was starting to see the value of keeping her clothes on.

It was chilly in the cabin, so Bolan just climbed under the quilt, and was asleep as soon as his head hit the pillow.

THE NEXT MORNING, they both awakened at the same time, when the sun came streaming through the log cabin's lone window.

Stretching his back enough to crack his spine, Bolan said, "I need to rent a boat and some diving equipment. Is there someone you trust we can do that with?"

"What do you mean, 'I'?"

"Just what I said. You've been a help, Lola, but I need to finish this by myself."

"By diving to this Castro's Lawn thingie by yourself?"

"Yes."

"You *are* a certified diver, right?"

"Of course."

"And you know that you're not supposed to go diving all alone, right?"

"You're also not supposed to shoot people without due process," Bolan pointed out. "What're you getting at?"

"I know every dive shop in the Keys, and none of them will rent you equipment solo. If you rent with me, then they'll do it, but no way otherwise." She stepped closer to him—she was angry. "Look, you took the certification, so you know the drill. You do *not* go diving without a buddy. A thousand different things can go wrong underwater, and that's before we meet the gunrunners. You want the boat and the scuba gear, I go with you. Period."

Bolan simply said, "Fine."

Within an hour, they had arrived at a dive shop run by a perky young woman who apparently hadn't seen Maxwell in far too long.

As she was negotiating for the renting of two full sets of diving gear and a boat, the woman leaned in to whisper something to her.

Then Maxwell turned to look at Bolan. "You do have your DAN card, right?"

Naturally, he carried whatever fake ID he felt he

might need over the course of a mission in a wallet, including his Divers Alert Network card.

He pulled out his wallet, removed the card and showed it to the woman behind the desk, and all was well.

The Executioner understood where both Maxwell and the woman who ran the dive shop were coming from. Scuba diving was a very heavily self-regulated hobby, which kept it from having to be regulated by outsiders like the government. The diving community was usually a small, tight one, and shops would never, under any circumstances, allow someone to dive unsafely.

As it was, it took Maxwell's considerable powers of persuasion to allow the pair of them to rent the boat without one of the shop's employees running the dive. Both Bolan and Maxwell had instructor certification on their DAN cards, which helped with that argument.

Once the arrangements were taken care of, they both had to take equipment that fit them. For Bolan it was relatively easy, but Maxwell had a much harder time of it. Most female divers were small and svelte, two words that assuredly did not apply to Maxwell. She even tried a men's size, but that was far too small in the chest.

Eventually, though, they found a neoprene wet suit that fit her.

After all that was taken care of, they were led to the boat, which was called the *Saint Marie*. It was a standard dive boat, a twenty-two-foot Burpee, that could probably hold up to eight divers, plus crew. It was more than enough for the two of them.

Bolan had been certified on these craft in his Army days, and Maxwell grew up in the Keys and could pilot pretty much any boat that sailed these waters, so they took turns taking the helm while the other kept an eye out for Dessens and checked over the equipment one last time.

"Look," Maxwell said suddenly at one point, "I wanted to thank you. I know I've been a pain in the ass, and I know it was stupid to sleep with Johnny, but…" She sighed, then smiled. "I appreciate you letting me be your dumb-but-loyal sidekick for this mission."

"What concerns me," Bolan said, not returning the smile, "is how seriously you *don't* take the work."

Maxwell shrugged. "Blame growing up down here. In the Keys, everyone's pretty devil may care. It's hard to take much of anything seriously when the most important thing in the world is to sit around in the sun and drink beer and eat fish."

"There's more to life than that," Bolan said, thinking of the lives ruined by people who placed themselves above the law. "Much more."

Within ninety minutes, they were closing in on the coordinates for Castro's Lawn.

There was already a yacht holding position at those coordinates, with a red-and-white diver's flag flying. From this distance, it looked empty, but the flag signaled that there were people diving. Anyone who passed by would think they were just a bunch of divers checking out the coral reefs that the area was famous for.

"Looks like Dessens is already here," Bolan said.

"At least she hasn't gotten away yet," Maxwell said. They had both been concerned that Dessens would have already cleared out by the time they got out there. But leaving before morning wasn't an option—they both needed the sleep, and navigating and diving in darkness was suicide, especially in this barren area of the Gulf of Mexico. Modern technology—GPS and computerized navigation, and so forth—could only get you so far if you couldn't see where the hell you were going.

This morning, though, was clear and sunny and warm. Perfect for a dive.

And for justice.

"There are two crates on the deck," Bolan said, pointing at the *Grant.* "My guess is they're moving them up in stages. That would mean there are still eight to go."

Maxwell nodded. "Let's do it."

They were already wearing their neoprene suits and headgear. Now that they'd arrived, they had to put on the rest: waterproof holsters for their weapons—the Desert Eagle for Bolan, the Beretta for Lola—flippers, face mask, breather and the air tank. That last was a heavy metal tank that strapped onto the back, and was all that stood between the diver and drowning.

After one final check to make sure the tanks were full and working, they both fell into the cool embrace of the Gulf of Mexico.

While it was nice and toasty warm above the water, the water itself was still quite chilly—hence the need for full neoprene suits. In more tropical regions, such as Hawaii or in the islands between Asia and Australia, the water got warm enough that you could dive in a bathing suit, but the Gulf never got that temperature.

Bolan took a brief moment to enjoy what he saw around him.

Maxwell did the same. When she told people she was a diver, they would nod and say, "Oh yeah, I've gone snorkeling a few times myself," as if that meant anything. Saying you know about scuba diving because you've gone snorkeling is akin to saying you know about skydiving because you've jumped off a low tree branch.

Snorkeling gave a hint, but it was just a preview of the main event. When you really went underwater, there were so many different shapes, sizes and colors. Maxwell knew that nothing on land came remotely close to the splendor one saw from the fish, reefs, plants and coral under the Gulf of Mexico. The fish loved to dart around and toward and under and over divers.

The thing that had impressed Maxwell the most, though, was the freedom. While it was true that you had to keep track of bottom time, air intake, surface intervals and so on, after a few dives, that was all done automatically, and you could just enjoy the freedom of movement. It was like what floating in zero gravity had to be like, except the water covered you like the world's biggest flannel blanket.

Eventually, they saw a large globe near the bottom. This was a particularly shallow stretch of the Gulf, so it wasn't all that deep, though they were past the depth where nitrogen narcosis was a risk.

According to the specs Brognola had e-mailed to Bolan the night before, there was an airlock on the top of the base that allowed people to readjust to the surface-normal pressure inside.

To their relief, the airlock was not in use, which meant that Dessens and whoever she had brought along were still packing up some number of the remaining eight crates.

From the outside, the airlock operated quite simply. Bolan pushed a big button lit in red, which then switched to yellow after he'd pressed it. Then they waited for it to turn green. When it did so, the door slid open slowly, water from the Gulf pouring into a small chamber of about twenty square feet. They swam in, and then Bolan pushed a similar-looking green-lit button on the inside. It changed to yellow as the door over their heads closed.

The button remained yellow while the water drained out of the chamber, and both the Executioner and Maxwell could feel the pressure lessening.

It was about a full minute after the water was drained that the button turned green, and a door perpendicular to the one they swam in slid slowly open.

Removing their tanks, masks, flippers and breathers, Bolan and Maxwell opened their waterproof holsters and brought their weapons to bear.

The airlock opened onto a catwalk that looked out over the main section of the base. Looking down, the Executioner saw banks of twenty-year-old computers: long, wide white monitors, thick white keyboards, ungainly CPUs, disk drives. All were inactive, of course.

Several chains with hooks on the ends were bound up near the ceiling. When unbound, the chains lowered to floor level. These were used for quick delivery of items from the airlock down to the main level.

On either side of the large chamber were two doors. One, he knew, led to barracks. The other likely led to a cargo hold.

At the end of the catwalk was a freight elevator that went down to the door to the cargo hold. Bolan pointed at it; Maxwell nodded.

They moved slowly down the catwalk.

Bolan whirled his head sharply at the sound of scuffling feet below him just as he pressed for the elevator.

Looking down, he saw two men, one with wild black

hair and a beard—and a yarmulke—wearing two bandoliers of grenades and holding a P90 TR personal defense weapon. Next to him was a man with a gray crew cut and a hard face, armed with a Heckler & Koch MP-7 A-1. They were moving a large wheeled dolly that had two crates on it. The crates were identical to the two on the *Grant's* deck.

Bolan dived off to the side, knocking Maxwell down with him, as both men opened fire. Rounds clanged off the catwalk railing, a couple sinking into flesh. Bolan felt the 4.6 mm rounds tear into the flesh of his right arm.

Ignoring the pain, he gripped the Desert Eagle with both hands and fired straight ahead. The .357 rounds he fired through the white-hot pain in his arm tore through the leather straps that bound the chains, but did no damage to the chains themselves, as they were made of sterner stuff.

But since the chains were unrestrained, they fell prey to gravity, their hooked ends hurtling toward the main level.

The two men saw what the Executioner had done, and stopped firing so they could drop to their knees and bring their hands up to protect their faces.

MARTY ANDERSON heard the gunfire and raced from the cargo hold to see what was going on.

Anderson hated guns—which was ironic, given his line of work since leaving the CIA. Indeed, his hatred of such weaponry was why he was initially so reluctant to join Dessens in her new career, though he was eventually lured with the promise of sex in the Bahamas with the woman of his dreams.

However, for all his hatred of guns, he was good with them. He'd always gotten good range scores, and he'd even had to threaten to shoot a real person once, though the man gave in before it got that far, to Anderson's relief. He'd never actually fired the Walther PPK that Dessens had given him when they started this job.

And now he never would.

As soon as he ran out of the cargo hold door, one of the chains that Bolan's Desert Eagle had freed from captivity came down right over the door. The end of the hook caved in Anderson's skull.

AFTER WATCHING the man who'd just entered the room get taken out by the hook, one of the men who'd been pushing the dolly said, "Son of a gee dash dee damn bitch! You're gonna die for that, mister, you hear me? Ain't that right, Conlon?"

"Yeah, Raviv."

As he shouted his threat, the bearded man named Raviv yanked a grenade off his bandolier, removed the pin and tossed the bomb up to the catwalk. It landed on the grille floor with a metallic clang.

Bolan and Maxwell both saw the grenade coming, and they dived in opposite directions, Bolan toward the elevator, Maxwell toward the airlock. Both raised their arms to protect themselves.

The shrapnel that the grenade spewed when it exploded wound up not harming either of them.

The catwalk itself, though, was another matter. The grenade's detonation had weakened the catwalk's support struts, and it started to buckle. Bolan leaped for the elevator, which had just arrived in response to his pressing the button moments earlier.

Maxwell was not so lucky.

Her end of the catwalk collapsed completely without the full support of the now-damaged struts, and she went hurtling toward the main chamber.

As she fell, she managed to squeeze off one round from her Beretta, but it ricocheted off the chains and hit one of the old computer monitors. The glass of the screen and the tube inside shattered, a small flame erupting from the impact.

For her part, Maxwell went limp in the hopes that it would minimize the impact, though it was probably like spitting in the ocean at this point.

Her body struck the metal floor of the base with a bone-crunching impact. Several ribs shattered, one piercing her lung. The bones of her left leg, which hit first, shattered into a dozen pieces. Miraculously, the femoral artery remained intact, but many other veins were punctured. Her left arm fared even worse, as the limb twisted the wrong way around as she landed, utterly mangling her ulna.

Bolan saw what had happened to Maxwell as the elevator door closed and swore vengeance.

As soon as the elevator opened, Bolan—standing once again in *sanchin* stance—squeezed off four rounds with his Desert Eagle.

Conlon, the second man who'd been moving the crates, fell, clutching his shredded leg as the first bullet did to his thigh what the grenade did to the catwalk.

The second bullet flew over his head, as did the third.

The fourth hit the bearded man, Raviv, in the left shoulder, instantly vaporizing his scapula and acromion, severing the connection to his humerus. His left arm fell to the floor, no longer attached to his body.

It appeared the man was trying to form words but was unable to. Instead he screamed.

Since he was the one who'd thrown the grenade that killed Maxwell, Bolan let him scream, unable to find mercy.

He hadn't been thrilled with Maxwell on this mission, but she'd done her part, and she certainly didn't deserve such a fate.

Exiting the elevator, the Executioner fired another shot at Conlon, who was trying to raise his H&K. Bolan's bullet pierced his cheek. Death came a moment later.

Raviv continued to scream, but Bolan ignored him.

Yvonne Dessens was the one he wanted.

"Don't move."

Bolan cursed himself. He should have spared Raviv a mercy round—his screams covered Dessens's movements enough so that he hadn't heard her come up from behind him.

"Right now," she said, "I'm pointing an OD Green Glock 19 right at your chest. If you budge, a 9 mm round is going to turn your heart into a thing of the past."

Bolan did not move.

Nor did he speak.

The next move was hers.

"I gotta tell you, mister—whoever you are—I don't know whether to shoot you or hire you."

"Go with your first instinct," Bolan said. "There is not a single circumstance under which I would work for a traitress like you."

"'Traitress'? Oh, how old-fashioned of you. For the record, 'traitor' is a non-gender-specific term. In any case, I was the one who was betrayed."

"I read your file," Bolan said dismissively. "Your job

was to serve your country. It wasn't up to you to question how your superiors decided to let you do that."

"'Let' me? Oh, that's rich. You know how many people died in New York in the fall of 2001? That could've been prevented if someone had just *listened* to me. But no, I'm just some dumb lady, what do *I* know?"

"So you decided to deal your own death in revenge?"

That brought Dessens up short. "What do you mean?"

"You think these guns you sell are being used for lawn ornaments? This shipment you've got here was originally tagged for a drug dealer."

"The guns exist, mister. Whether I'm here or not, slimeballs like Rico will still get their hands on them. I may as well take advantage of the process, my connections and make some cash for myself."

"If you're trying to justify yourself to me, give it up. I'm not interested."

"Yes, but I'm interested in you. Before you arrived in Florida, everything was going swimmingly. Now it's a couple of days later, and my entire organization is pretty much gone. So I need to know—who are you?"

"Get used to disappointment, Ms. Dessens. It's over."

"I'm the one with the gun at your back."

"And I'm the one who took down Lee, Delgado, Jiminez, Martinez, Hawkins, Brand, Favre, and some others whose names I don't know, not to mention the six men you sent to kill us and the three corpses on the floor right now."

Only then did Bolan realize that Raviv had stopped screaming. The Executioner hoped that meant that he was finally dead.

"One of those corpses is my assistant, Marty. He never hurt a fly."

"If he was your assistant, he's as complicit as you."

"I meant him personally. He was a good man, a kind man and very well organized. I couldn't have done this without him. And he was always so grateful to me." Her tone sounded briefly wistful. "But enough of this. I ask again, who are you?"

"And I say again, get used to disappointment. You'll die never knowing who I am."

"You're just trying to get me to shoot you before I can interrogate you properly." She chuckled. "I had really thought Perry and his people would be able to handle it, once I got word that you and Maxwell were staying in the Summerland Key safehouse. Ah, well."

Before Bolan could mull on what those words meant, he heard a whoosh sound. Glancing to his left, he saw that a small fire had started, and was spreading. It looked like the monitor that Maxwell's ricochet had destroyed had conflagrated.

"Oh great," Dessens said, "a fire. Well, I was gonna destroy this place anyhow. Raviv's explosives would've been faster." With a dramatic sigh, she aimed her Glock center mass. "It was nice knowing you, mister—but it's all over now."

The Executioner saw the muzzle-flash of a pistol out of the corner of his eye. A bullet whizzed through the air and struck its intended target, shredding bone and heart muscle. Blood spewed from the wound, escaping the body in life-threatening amounts, as the heart could no longer pump it to where it was needed in the body.

And Yvonne Dessens fell to the floor of Castro's Lawn, dead.

Whirling, Bolan saw that Maxwell had managed to

raise her Beretta one last time to shoot the woman who'd ordered the death of her lover.

Bolan ran to her side, but by the time he got there, the light had gone out of her eyes. Her dead, bloody face stared upward at the chains that now dangled from the ceiling of the base.

Warm air pushed against Bolan's head, and he realized that the fire was spreading. There was no time to get anyone's body out of there. Maxwell deserved a proper burial, but a watery grave was probably sufficiently dramatic to suit her.

Getting back to his feet, Bolan ran toward the elevator.

"Hey…hey ass…asshole!"

The ragged voice was coming from the floor behind him. Turning, Bolan saw that Raviv wasn't quite dead yet.

"Set—set all the—the charges a'ready."

The Executioner saw that Raviv was holding, fittingly, a dead-man's switch and had pushed the button.

As soon as he expired, he'd let go of it, and whatever charges he'd set would go off.

Bolan turned and ran, increasing his pace to the elevator.

As soon as it got him to the upper level, his heart sank, as there was a twenty-foot gap between the intact part of the catwalk and the airlock entrance.

Moving to the rear of the elevator to give himself as much of a running start as possible, he leaped across the abyss, barely managing to gain purchase on the shredded metal of the catwalk segment that was still connected to the airlock entrance.

His diver's hood was impaled on one of those shredded bits of metal, and only then did Bolan realize that his mask, breather and air tank, as well as those of

Maxwell, had all fallen to the floor when the catwalk was destroyed.

There was no way he'd have time to go back down and find the diving equipment.

Raviv would be dead any minute, and Bolan would join him a second later.

Slamming his hand on the button, the airlock opened and Bolan crawled in.

He took half-a-dozen deep breaths in order to saturate his lungs with oxygen.

Even as he did so, he knew that wasn't the risk. When you held your breath, it wasn't the lack of oxygen that did you in, but the buildup of carbon dioxide. Worse, he was going to have to swim back up to the surface without making a safety stop to shed excess nitrogen, which meant he risked nitrogen narcosis—a particular problem when he had to operate the *Saint Marie* when he got to the surface.

But nitrogen narcosis was better than dead.

He hit the button.

The airlock started to fill with water, and Bolan took a few more deep breaths, saving the final one that he held for when the water was at his chin level.

The worst part of the wait was having to tread water in the airlock while he waited for the pressure to equalize.

As soon as the button turned green, he squeezed out of the slowly opening airlock door and swam for all he was worth.

Survival was reduced to the imperative of windmilling his arms and pumping his legs to propel him faster, ever faster, toward the surface.

When he caught sight of the sun poking through the water, he knew he was close.

Then the base exploded.

Several tons of displaced water shot upward, carrying Bolan on the shock wave. He burst through the surface in the middle of a massive water spout. He opened his mouth, expelling the deadly carbon dioxide, but not daring to inhale until he was out of the water.

He also let his body go limp, hoping that when he came back down onto the surface of the Gulf, it wouldn't be hitting a brick wall.

In fact, it was more like hitting a wooden wall: still very very painful. Bolan managed to get himself to float on the newly choppy water in his neoprene suit, his body feeling like one entire bruise. But with his head above water once again, he was able to breathe.

He stayed that way for the better part of a minute, getting his breathing under control.

Then he rolled himself ninety degrees and started treading water, even though fatigue made his limbs feel like they were made of lead. He caught sight of both the *Grant* and the *Saint Marie*. As he swam toward the latter, he thought about the eight crates that had been destroyed beneath the sea, and the two left on Dessens's boat.

According to Danny Delgado, those weapons had been designated for destruction. Belatedly, that order had been carried out for eight of the ten crates, thanks to the Executioner's actions. He intended to make sure that it happened for the other two as well.

Clambering into the *Saint Marie,* he paused to get his breath under control once again.

Instead, he passed out.

Epilogue

Bolan came to on the bed in the Summerland Key safe-house, with Brognola standing over him.

"Good to see that you're okay, Striker."

Bolan tried to sit up, but Brognola put a gentle hand on his clavicle.

"Not so fast there, Striker. We've got a doctor coming to look at you."

"Not yet," Bolan said, gently brushing the hand aside. "I appreciate your concern, Hal, but the mission's not done yet."

"I had the Coast Guard check up on the coordinates of Castro's Lawn when you didn't check in. They're still sifting through the wreckage, but they've found the remains of at least four people, one of whom is definitely Dessens, and another one of whom is Maxwell, unfortunately. All the major players are dead. The gun ring's broken, and you've done your duty. Now you can resume your R and R in Michigan."

"Not quite," Bolan said. Only when he gingerly rose to his feet did he realize that he was only wearing a pair of briefs. He assumed that the Coast Guard had removed his neoprene.

Walking to the closet, he took out some clothes to change into.

"I have one more stop to make, Hal. Only three people should've known that Maxwell and I were in this safehouse—the two of us, and you. I know you didn't betray us, and I know there's no official record of us being there."

"Yeah, but Dessens—" Then Brognola got it. "There's no way, even if she had her old access, she'd know we were there."

"Unless it's from someone who saw us here."

"You think that stripper…?"

Bolan shook his head as he shrugged into a button-down shirt. "No. Erica was a free agent that Delgado used for his own ends. I doubt Dessens even knew who she was."

"Then who?"

Rather than answer the question, Bolan said simply as he buttoned his shirt, "I need to contact someone in the DEA."

MARCUS FONTAINE SAT in his apartment in Hialeah, waiting for a phone call that would never come.

He'd done what he was supposed to do, and now Dessens was supposed to call *him* and tell him where to pick up the money.

It was just one gambling debt. That was all. Fontaine had never really gone much for gambling until a coworker took him to one of the Indian casinos, and now he was hooked.

Mostly everything had been fine, until he went into that Texas Hold 'Em no-limit game. He had pocket Aces, and he figured he was golden, especially since that other guy stayed in after the other player who was left in the tournament folded.

Two more Aces showed up on the flop, and Fontaine knew that he had it in the bag. Only thing that could beat him was a straight flush, and the makings for that weren't on the board unless you had a two and a five suited in your hand. But nobody in their right mind would bet with that shitty a hand, so Fontaine knew all was well.

His opponent went all in. But knowing he just had to be bluffing, Fontaine, who had fewer chips than the gentleman, went all in also.

He had the two and the five suited to get the straight flush.

Fontaine couldn't believe it. He'd been betting aggressively *before* the flop—but it was a stone cold bluff.

Fontaine, who could stand in a room with hard-core drug kingpins and know exactly when they were telling the truth, had had no idea that this jackass had been bluffing out his ass.

But the buy in for the tournament had been ten grand, which Fontaine didn't actually have. So he borrowed it, figuring he'd have no problem with the winnings, seeing as his luck had been going so well.

After his big loss his luck only got worse. He couldn't even win at the damn slot machines, and his debt was accruing interest.

But he couldn't stop. Gambling had become his addiction.

Dessens then called him completely out of the blue, and offered to forgive his debt and keep him on her payroll—with the condition that he stayed with the DEA and fed her info when she needed it, or whenever he found something. He had a new habit to feed, so he said yes.

This week, he'd thought his luck was finally changing. Dessens had told her people in the area to be on the lookout for some ex-deputy chick named Maxwell, and had circulated a picture of the woman. When Fontaine heard that the Summerland Key safehouse would be unavailable for the next few days, he wondered if there might be a connection, and so he drove out to the safehouse and waited for the guests to arrive. His hunch was rewarded when Maxwell showed up with some guy. Fontaine casually left the house, got in his car and immediately called Dessens.

Dessens was very happy, and promised him twenty thousand dollars. Which was good, as the damn Bucs had blown the spread again.

But she hadn't called yet to give him a pickup for the cash.

In the year that Fontaine had been secretly working for her, Dessens had never missed a phone call. She was reliable that way.

Fontaine was startled by the buzz of the front doorbell.

Getting up, he walked over and buzzed the person in. The intercom had stopped working years ago, but he'd never worried about fixing it. He had always figured that criminals wouldn't ring the bell anyway, and he could always intimidate salespeople and Jehovah's Witnesses with his badge and-or weapon.

Fontaine opened the door, shocked to see the man from the safehouse walking up the stairs—the man he'd assumed was dead by now.

Confused, Fontaine feigned lightheartedness and said, "Shit, what are you doing here? You didn't believe my apartment was *really* that bad, did you?"

"May I come in?" Bolan asked.

Shrugging, Fontaine opened the door wider. "Sure, why not?"

Bolan entered, and Fontaine shut the door behind him. Moving toward the kitchen, he asked, "Can I get you something?"

"I'm fine," Bolan said.

"Well, if you want to hang out or something, that's fine, but I gotta warn you that I'm expecting a phone call that's kinda private, so—"

"Dessens won't be calling you, Agent Fontaine."

Fontaine suddenly developed a coughing fit. Once he got over it, he asked, "Excuse me?"

"The phone call you're expecting is from Yvonne Dessens, who will call you to—well, I'm not sure. Discuss the terms of your next assignment? Tell you how much she's paying you for giving up me and Lola Maxwell? Arrange payment through a Cayman Islands account?"

For a brief instant, Fontaine considered denying the charge.

But he realized that that was foolish. If this guy was alive and Dessens hadn't called, it meant that whatever she'd intended to do to the man standing in front of him had failed, and whatever he'd done to Dessens had succeeded.

"Actually," he said in a quiet, defeated voice, "she was gonna call to give me a drop for the cash. I don't have the clout for a Cayman Islands account, I'm just a working federal agent, y'know? So she gives me cash when I give her info."

"She's not giving anyone anything anymore, Agent Fontaine," Bolan said in a simple monotone. "She's dead. Her organization is broken. There's just one loose end to tie off."

Looking down, Fontaine shook his head.

"I just had some gambling debts, you know? Didn't think anybody would get hurt." He chuckled. "You familiar with Bruce Springsteen?"

"I've heard of him," Bolan said neutrally.

"He says in one of his songs that he has debts no honest man could pay. Well, I'm not an honest man anymore, but I've got debts. So I did what I did. And I guess now I gotta be paying for it."

Just then Fontaine quickly grabbed for something out of a kitchen drawer, but before he could properly aim his pistol, Bolan raised his SIG-Sauer and fatally shot Agent Fontaine in the head.

"Yeah, Agent Fontaine. Yeah, you do."

Moments later, Bolan walked out of an apartment building in Hialeah, having left a bloody corpse behind in Marcus Fontaine's apartment.

Fontaine was the final loose end. The only other people who worked for Yvonne Dessens's gunrunning ring who still drew breath were too low-level to be of consequence. They were the types who'd either get killed on the streets, get arrested on an aggravated assault or murder charge, or get sick of the life and get out.

Jean-Louis Faraday died of a postoperative infection. Bolan would attend his funeral, as well as that of Lola Maxwell, if he could.

The only person who got a happy ending out of it was Erica "Star" Mayes. Before he died at the Executioner's hand, Danny Delgado had given Erica the money he'd promised her. So she was ten grand richer, and able to take a hiatus from Hot Keys the following semester and get her degree that much sooner.

She'd also broken up with Xavier.

Walking a few blocks through Miami, Bolan eventually got to the spot where he'd parked Maxwell's cherry-red 1965 Mustang. He'd picked it up from the mechanic that morning—it had been restored, good as new.

Turning the engine over, it purred like a content cat. Bolan put it into gear and drove off.

Eventually, he was going to drive the car back to Lola Maxwell's place. He was sure that one of her relatives would claim the car when her estate was settled.

For now, though, he was going to have a final joy ride in it. He suspected that Maxwell would've wanted it that way.